NIGHT STRIKE

A RED BRANCH MISSION
BOOK 1

BLAZE WARD

KNOTTED ROAD PRESS

Night Strike
A Red Branch Mission: 1
Blaze Ward
Copyright © 2024 Blaze Ward
All rights reserved
Published by Knotted Road Press
www.KnottedRoadPress.com

ISBN: 978-1-64470-429-5

Cover and interior design copyright © 2024 Knotted Road Press

Reviews
It's true. Reviews help. Even a short one, such as, "Loved it!" So please consider reviewing this book (and all of the ones you've read) on your favorite retailer site.

Never miss a release!
If you'd like to be notified of new releases, sign up for my newsletter.

http://www.blazeward.com/newsletter/

Buy More!
Did you know that you can buy directly from the Knotted Road Press website?

https://www.knottedroadpress.com/shop/

This book is licensed for your personal enjoyment only. All rights reserved. This is a work of fiction. All characters and events portrayed in this book are fictional, and any resemblance to real people or incidents is purely coincidental. This book, or parts thereof, may not be reproduced in any form without permission.

ALSO BY BLAZE WARD

The Science Officer Series

Start with: The Science Officer

The Jessica Keller Chronicles

Start with: Auberon

CS-405 (Command Centurion Kosnett, part of Jessica)

Start with: Queen Anne's Revenge

First Centurion Kosnett (sequel to Jessica)

Start with: Encounter at Vilahana

Additional Alexandria Station Stories

Alexandria Station Collection

Handsome Rob (Alexandria Station Universe)

Start with: Can't Shoot Straight Gang

=====================

Corsac Fox

Start with: Flight of the Corsac Fox

Operation Marrakesh

Start with: Trial by Leviathan

Captain Daring

Start with: Revoked

The Hunter Bureau

Start with: Mirrors

Fairchild

Start with: Fairchild

Last Stand

Start with: Lost Dreams

The Lazarus Alliance

Start with: Escape

Shadow of the Dominion

Start with: Longshot Hypothesis

Star Dragon

Start with: Birth of the Star Dragon

Kincaide's War

Start with: The Eden Package

Star Tribes

Start with: Winterstar

Blaze also writes Action-Adventure Here

Special thanks to Ken Burnside, Philip Markgraf, and Ethan McKinney for letting me tap their expertise. All the mistakes are still going to be mine, but their help hopefully meant a lot fewer of them.

ESSAY: WHY THE RED BRANCH?

I enjoy writing and reading action. Motion. Energy. Adventure. Let's start there.

I do not read a lot. I know that some folks demand that anyone writing needs to read ten times (or more) as much as they write, but I have a different approach. (Which is a polite way of saying that it might work for them, but that they are utterly wrong for me. Don't tell me I MUST do anything, bubbles.)

I write the stories I want to read. The ones that I can't find anywhere else because nobody else is writing them. It goes back to when the Fabulous Publisher Babe™ first convinced me that I could write fiction and make money at it, which was a novel revelation to me in 2013.

I knew a lot of starving artist authors. Still do. But the world had changed, and you could make money without Traditional Publishing, so I gave it a try.

Then one Sunday afternoon, we're in Powell's books, in Beaverton, Oregon. She's part of a large group of writers doing a mass signing event, and I'm support staff, because nobody knows who I am. (They still don't, but that mostly me flying under the radar as much as possible.)

Folks have gotten set up and we're all killing time. I'm walking up and down long rows of SF/F aisles with money burning a hole in the my pocket, and I can't find a single book that I actually want to buy, new or used. Because nobody was writing them at the time, it seemed.

(Turns out Indie was, but Indie tends to be ebook heavy and not paper, so the bookstores don't really know us.)

I complained to the Babe about my problem, and her response kinda set me on this path. Technically, that means I get to blame her. Heh.

"So write it," she said.

Well, shit. Duh.

So I did. That was Auberon. Military SF with a badass woman commander who wasn't helpless or wimpy or weak or dumb. Competence porn, if you know what that means. I have described her more than once as a gender-swapped Jim Kirk without the libido, and that's as accurate as anything.

So, I wrote it. And it sold. And still sells.

And it taught me that I can write the stories I want to read. Which brings us to the Red Branch.

I was looking up costumed superheroes on wikipedia one night, because I use that website and tvtropes.org as points of research and inspiration. Rabbit-holing, we call it, because you just keep wandering down the various links until you have exhausted the question, or found the answer you need.

In the process, I found a reference to a comic book I had a few issues of from when I was a kid. (Late 70s, vintage, bought used from comic book store maybe 1981 or so.)

Blackhawk.

By the point I found them, they had gone through several iterations, and were in their jet-fighter spy-mercenary phase, right before they were canceled in 1977, but they had started out in 1941 (Pre-US Entry into WW2) as a group of mercenary pilots fighting Nazis and other evildoers during the war, before shit got a little (or a lot) weird in the Fifties and Sixties.

At one point in those early days, as I researched closer, I discovered that Blackhawk the comic was usually the second or third selling title in any given month, behind Action (Superman) as #1 and would swap with Wonder Woman for second place depending on sales.

Huge. They did a movie serial in the 1950s, but it was not good. Let's just leave it at that. And the publisher went out of business in '56, with DC taking over and trying new ideas. None of them really worked. Eventually, they reverted to the 40s and the war and come and go, with "modern" incarnations being kids or grandkids or something. I don't read comics these days so I am only a Casual.

But the idea hooked me. And I started doing research to set something after the war, because I wanted jets and those only started to come into action at the very end, when Germany had already lost and was trying anything to survive.

But post-war, there are jets. The Gloster Meteor and the de Havilland Vampire. And I started getting deep into the research, discovering where the Brits had licensed jet engines to the Soviet Union in 1947, which got copied and improved.

And I sat down and drew on my political science and history background, and decided that the Soviets would happily hunt escaped Nazis after the war, but would be limited by the Iron Curtain and all that.

It all came together with a Blackhawk-like group of Soviet pilots, exiled from home and trying to make a living as mercenaries in the West. Deep cover. Hiding in plain sight. And the Ratlines the Catholic Church set up and the US Army (probably) ignored got a lot of terrible people to South America. The Americans also employed a lot of people who probably should have been hung from the neck until dead, if you look closely enough at what they did before 1946.

Some really icky fuckers.

So I have ex-Soviet pilots hunting war criminals while having dogfights and all sorts of excitement. Five-man-band tropes and history.

I try not to use real people, even dead ones, except in

extraordinary circumstances. These novels are the things that happen along the sides and don't get a lot of publicity, except when Sasha and the team have to step up and stop true evil.

Which brings me to the Werewolf Legion. A group of Nazis who weren't the major war criminals who were ignored in order to stop communism, but were all still soundly committed to the entire concept of Nazism and everything that Hitler demanded.

Also mercenaries, because folks like Peron really didn't like the US government throwing its weight around and were happy to let in all those folks who wanted to start a new life and were willing to try Argentina and other places to do it.

And one of those late-war Hitler superweapons that never got beyond the talking shop phase resonated with me as a threat to world peace. The Amerikabomber was supposed to take off from Germany, bomb New York City or Washington, DC, and return home. A terror weapon, because they couldn't have built more than one or a handful by that point, but they wanted Americans to understand what it felt like to be bombed in your own home.

So Voss and Gerstenberger needed to build one. I got inspired by that beast flying wing from the first Captain America movie, which was itself inspired by the Northrop YB-49 flying wing (jet version of the YB-35), which built on what the Horton Brothers were doing during the war.

Flying wings work, if you want slow and efficient long range. The American B-2 ad B-21 bombers have proven that, but it really requires computerized reflexes to maintain, because the flight characteristics can get screwy fast if you aren't careful in the design phase.

It will, however, let you take off from Argentina and bomb New York City if you do it right. Won't destroy the city, but it will panic people, and if you conduct the right kind of night strike, you could even get away afterwards and return home.

Doing so in 1948, however, might have started World War III, at a time when the US had sole capability to use nuclear weapons and a lot of people wanted to use that power to annihilate the

Communist Menace™ entirely. Thankfully, we never got there, but it walked right up to the edge more than once. As I research, I'm still not entirely sure how the Berlin Airlift never triggered a shooting war, other than the East Germans were apparently bluffing and Stalin refused to escalate when the Americans pushed back.

But these were dangerous times, and a group of pilots will be forced to decide whether or not they should save their mortal enemy from an attack by a group of dead-ender Nazis.

Heroes will rise. Even from the unlikeliest of places.

And a new adventure will begin.

AIRCRAFT RESEARCH: THE NIGHT-FIGHTER

Let's talk about the difference between a dayfighter and an all-weather fighter, what was sometimes called a night-fighter in those days. Most fighter aircraft were one-man jobbies, intended to be fast and maneuverable, so they could dogfight with other fighters or chase down bombers and shoot them out of the sky.

Day bombing requires massive fleets of bombers, all heavily armed and flying in tight formations where hopefully all those defensive guns can protect you. Didn't always work, because the German defenders could get high, then dive through the formation at high speed, blasting as they went. Serious casualties resulted., until American fighter designs had the fuel to go from Britain to Berlin and back, at which point they could escort the bombers.

That's day fighting. Night fighting is a whole other beast.

The British functionally invented Radar as we know it for military uses, and could spot German bombers coming in time to vector the RAF into place to intercept. Even at night.

None of the one-man fighters could carry a primitive radar system, because they were huge in those days. Someone had to spot things and radio you what you needed.

But they could mount radars on larger craft. The Bristol Beaufighter was originally intended as a Heavy Fighter, meaning twin engines and a lot of guns, but it turned out to be fast and maneuverable. And carried a stupendous amount of firepower, with four 20mm cannon in the nose and up to 6 .303 machine-guns on the wings.

More importantly, early radar could be mounted, meaning that the aircraft could see others at night. It's dark up there at night, which is why you see those enormous spotlights in old movies, trying to light up enemy aircraft so fighters or anti-aircraft guns can hit them.

I started there. The de Havilland Vampire is a two-seater jet that was remarkably maneuverable for its odd shape. Possibly had a bit of Area Rule going, long before Whitcomb formalized his ideas.

More importantly, there was a radar-equipped nightfighter version, the DH.113. This made it capable of fighting both during daylight hours and after dark, which made it one of the first jet-fighter night-fighters. These days, those are called All-Weather fighters, but that's just being able to track targets in rain and snow as well as clear skies.

It gave me a team of expert pilots who could do things day and night, because you can get a lot sneakier after sunset. Oddly, the Soviet Union didn't really build a competent night-fighter until much later, but they had a system where radar operators on the ground would vector pilots in manually instead of putting the tools on the aircraft. This will show up later and bite them on the ass, but the Americans weren't really much better, maintaining the propellor-driven Northrop P-61 Black Widow in service long after they should have been retired, often stripping planes for parts to repair others because they weren't building the Lockheed F-94 Starfire (in service May 1950) or the Northrop F-89 Scorpion (in service Sept 1950) until later, and had a lot of teething problems to work out.

The MiG-15 and the F-86 Sabre were day-fighters, pure and simple. Amazingly fast and maneuverable, but blind at night without a lot of help.

So I started with the Vampire and imagined those jet engines the Brits licensed to the Soviets, which eventually got improved into the Klimov VK-1. Let's put a pair of a slightly earlier design in a Vampire. And upgrade the cannons. And leave the ability to bomb by adding wingtip tanks and drop tanks.

For the era, the Nightviper as it could have been built would have been amazing. Of course, nobody was doing things like that. They wanted fast and heavy and daytime. Nuclear missiles don't really become a thing for another decade, so bombers had to carry nuclear weapons. Or surface to surface missiles like the MGM-1 Matador (in service 1952).

Bombers could carry radar systems. And in early jet bombers, the goal was to go as fast and as high as possible, to avoid interception by aircraft (this was before surface-to-air self-guiding missiles that could shoot them down).

I wanted an all-around weapon, in the hands of my experts. Dogfighting at altitude. Faster than any piston-driven aircraft. Able to bomb at low levels because I included a woman test pilot from The Night Witches.

And they had a competent jet that was as good or better than anything in the sky in 1948. But, as I have noted elsewhere, every year 1946-1956 brought a revolution in air power, as things got better, so the Nightviper is only going to be good enough for a time. Then it will be replaced. And that's its own story for a later volume.

For now, enjoy Night Strike, and the start of an adventure.

PART ONE
SPY

CHAPTER 1

William crushed out the cigarette and checked his wristwatch as two quiet raps on the door interrupted his afternoon. Outside the window, Buenos Aires had fallen into that mid-day lull where folks slowed for a time, before building up the mad energy of evening.

Not his favorite city, or even country, but the money was simply too good to pass up.

He checked the Government Issue Colt .45 holstered under his left arm as he rose, not bothering to button his blazer. William doubted that he'd need to quickdraw this afternoon, but some habits died hard.

Plus, the man at the door had been his mortal enemy until only a few years ago. And had many enemies of his own. They might have even remained deadly foes, except that the American OSS had demobilized William just as quickly as they had gotten rid of most of the soldiers that had liberated Europe from the Nazis.

Before letting so many of the important villains sneak away in the dead of night.

William rose and approached the door, off to one side in case someone was about to open fire through it. He'd gotten that one SS Major in Heidelheim that way.

"*¿Quien es?*" he called quietly, aware of how thin the walls were in this hotel.

Who is it?

Old place. Built in the Twenties when all the world was a party. Before the bills came due.

Not even Peron had been able to bring it all back, though he seemed intent on rescuing as many old Nazis as he could, regardless of what Washington or London thought.

Or maybe those cities were helping. The Catholic Church couldn't have done all this without a lot of folks intentionally looking the other way along that road, and William was on the outside these days. Scrambling to make a buck.

Even working with folks like this.

"Señor Zorro," a man replied just as quietly.

Mr. Fox.

William nodded to himself and undid the bolt, stepping behind the door to mostly hide as he opened it.

His guest slid in quickly and William closed it back up, setting the bolt again just in case. Wouldn't keep anyone out for long, but would at least give him enough time to draw and shoot if he had to.

Mr. Fox. A cute play on words, assuming you didn't know who the man really was. Didn't already recognize one of Nazi Germany's ace pilots at the end of the war. Not the best, but in the top ten who survived, after decade of war in Spain and then Europe.

Hauptmann Alois Voss, *vos* being another term for fox in German. Flying name: the Blue Wolf. Supposedly shot down and killed in the final days of the Battle of Berlin. Records even showed the man dead.

Obviously not.

And he fit *vos*, having a lean build with dancer's muscles and reddish hair kept slicked back with oil. Nice civilian suit today, with a brown leather briefcase in one hand and a snappy gray fedora on his head. Seeing him on the streets of Buenos Aires, you'd take him for another German emigre.

A massive number of those these days. Peron made no bones that he thought the whole Nuremberg thing a travesty of vengeance instead of justice.

But Peron wasn't exactly a leftie.

"Good afternoon, Mr. Fox," William nodded as he moved back to the table where he'd been sitting before.

Voss took up a spot close to the window, back and to one side where he could see, but not be seen. His briefcase stayed close when he put it down.

Like a man hiding from the world and ready to move quickly

"I got your telegram indicating success?" Voss glanced over.

"Indeed, sir," William replied. "I have many useful contacts, even today. And it was actually easier to get copies of Northrop's plans than it was to talk to Reimar Horton. That one lives in terror that American or Soviet agents will knock on his door at midnight and disappear him to work in some secret lab for the rest of his life."

"Pity," Voss nodded. "He would have been exactly the man to assist in my new project, but I suppose that we'll make do without him. Have you the plans ready to exchange?"

"I do," William brightened up. "The agreed amount?"

"Indeed," Voss said.

William watched the man reach into the left slit pocket on his blazer and pull out a thick envelope. He stepped close enough to hand it over, then retreated back to the window and watched.

William opened it and thumbed through a stack of US hundreds. Far more than he'd ever made as an OSS agent, but the American government was cheap that way. Hardly anything for retirement for three years of deadly danger.

What did they expect old spies to do after being thrown out?

William put the envelope in his blazer pocket and stood, going into the closet and pulling out the thick manila folder from where he'd hidden it earlier. Not impossible to find, but impossible to find quickly, in case someone had trailed him to South America.

Lots of traffic north and south these days. Easy to blend in, especially as so many folks built up new trade with the rising industrial powers of the southern hemisphere. Argentina would take its place next to America in another generation, it seemed.

William returned to the table and opened the folder, sliding out a variety of blueprints, as well as a set of microfiche films containing vast amounts of US Department of War reports and plans.

"Everything you need to update the old Horton H.XVIII in variants A, B, and C. Additionally, original plans for the Northrop XB-35 and YB-35, plus what they are doing right now to transform it into the jet-powered YB-49. One hell of a long-range transport, if they were to civilianize it, like you plan to do."

He watched the man take the packet and thumb randomly through pages and film, nodding to himself. William liked to think of himself as a patriot, but he also needed to eat, and the OSS had tossed him out on his ass without even a kiss goodbye.

If Voss and his people wanted to put Boeing or Douglas or McDonnell out of the civilian aviation business, that was their fault, wasn't it?

"Excellent, William," Voss smiled.

He moved to the briefcase and set it on the table, opening it up to file everything away.

A small part of William's professional training appreciated the sudden Walther P-38 with the long silencer on the end, even as it pointed at his chest.

"I'm sorry, William, but you know too much," Voss smiled sadly.

Then four quiet shots rang out and he heard only silence.

CHAPTER 2

Oliverio Hernandez was reviewing some dull contract language for a client when Maria opened the door to his small office and delivered the morning newspaper with the mail.

"It's terrible, what's happening these days," she shook her head.

"What's that?" he asked, looking up befuddled for a moment.

Maria often had opinions on things, but mostly they were nothing more than a middle-aged woman with little to look forward to, her normal disposition a bit too abrasive for most men and not the tall, slinky blonde that so many businessmen strove to acquire as mistresses these days.

Oliverio was fine with one wife and two children at home. He didn't need the added headache.

"A tourist murdered," she said, pointing to the lurid article down the right, interrupted with a line-drawing of an Anglo obviously reproduced from a passport photo. It had that bland edge that made everyone look bad. "Right here in Buenos Aires. What is the world coming to?"

"Terrible," he offered. "Could you find me the Gomez file while you're here? I was going to work on that next, and can save you the trip."

And get her out of his hair.

She hadn't been here that day. In fact, he had specifically given Maria that day off to go visit her sister, so that he could meet privately with William Jacobs. The pay had been good, for what amounted to a silly insurance policy like one might encounter in a lurid mystery thriller novel.

Except that someone had murdered Jacobs, just as the man had feared.

Oliverio took a moment to calm himself, nervous that whoever had killed the American might decide to track down all of Jacobs' loose ends. There shouldn't be any. The man had claimed to be a former American spy, and had explained some of the things he had called tradecraft.

The strange phone calls at odd hours. The meetings outside the office where he had to follow a scavenger hunt of clues to finally meet the man in person.

The letter that William Jacobs had entrusted to Oliverio's care.

If something were to happen...

Oliverio supposed that it had. He didn't need to know more. William had left him a small package, instructions, and paid cash ahead of time for Oliverio to act as something of an executor to his Last Will and Testament.

And Oliverio had intentionally not peeked. Didn't want to know. Didn't EVER want to know.

Especially as his instructions were to forward the package to the new Soviet embassy, relations having just been restored in 1946. With William's cover letter intact.

A deadman switch, the man had called it. Insurance policy in Oliverio's mind, but his client was dead. Murdered in his hotel room and nothing seemingly stolen, given the report in the paper.

Oliverio knew better. The other package had been stolen. Or delivered and William murdered to cover someone's trail.

Oliverio didn't want to know. He had to execute a Last Will and Testament. And then be done with it.

Hopefully forever.

CHAPTER 3

Sasha hadn't had more than a glass of vodka tonight. He hadn't gone out to a club looking for fun or trouble. Hadn't done hardly much of anything.

Dinner in the officer's commissary. By himself because several of the men in his flying squadron were planning to go out dancing tonight, and had skipped food. Had gotten themselves all cleaned up and showered into their best uniforms, looking for songbirds to seduce. Sasha—Major Aleksandr Kryvenko—had retired to his room instead, reading some classic English literature to keep in practice.

During the Great Patriotic War, his previous language training had seen him liaison with Western contacts, generally British and American, mostly delivering aircraft via Persia and the south, where they could be used to drive the Nazis back. Later, training young pilots, because someone had to, and he'd had a knack for it.

Finally, and only at the end, being part of the great air armadas crushing the fascists once and for all. Raining death and destruction on German towns a thousand-fold for Stalingrad and Leningrad and Moscow and a hundred other places put to the torch coming or going.

But tonight, a quiet night, in his room. Late in the day, but not so late that he was ready to sleep just yet. Reading.

The knock at the door surprised him. Everyone else was out, as far as he knew. He sighed and put his book down, next to the empty glass that had had his one vodka.

He pulled his tunic straight and walked to the door, opening it to a pair of strangers.

"Yes?" Sasha asked.

Both men were in civilian attire, which struck him as odd in the middle of a Red Army Air Base.

"Major Kryvenko?" the taller one asked.

Older of the two, but just past thirty when the other looked just shy, both several years younger than Sasha.

"That's right," he nodded. "What can I help you with?"

The older one flashed an identity card while the younger one drew a Tokarev semiautomatic pistol and pointed it at him.

"Aleksandr Kryvenko, you are under arrest as a spy against the Motherland," the leader said, jamming into the room and carrying Sasha backwards to the table.

He didn't resist, mostly out of shock, but also not wanting to be shot.

The man turned him around and cold metal cuffs closed on his wrists, the smell of bad Turkish cigarettes coming over his shoulder as the man leaned in.

"Do not resist or you will be shot," he said. "Am I clear?"

"What's going on?" Sasha asked.

"That is not for you to know, traitor."

They hustled him out of the room.

CHAPTER 4

Gennadi looked up when the door opened. He was surprised to see Comrade General Shuysky standing there, a thick folder in one hand and his Hero of the Soviet Union ribbon seemingly polished to a brighter glow today. Doubly so as Gennadi's aide Yefim hadn't opened the door for the man, though Gennadi could see his reliable assistant standing well behind the General in case there were orders.

Gennadi studied the General's face.

"Coffee," he said simply to his assistant, watching Yefim nod and vanish.

General Shuysky entered and sat heavily in the visitor's chair, closing the door as he did. Studied Gennadi with intense eyes.

"How is the arm, Colonel Nazarenko?" the man asked after a moment.

Gennadi shrugged.

"It will never be what it was," he said. "Some days, it works better than others, but my flying days are behind me. The cane already promised that. Hell, some days I cannot even drive, though the promise of an automatic transmission in a vehicle means that I might not be entirely deskbound for the rest of my life with no clutch or shifter to work."

He didn't mean for it to come out bitter. He had survived,

after all. Both the battle that had seen him crash in a fireball, as well as the Great Patriotic War that had destroyed the Fascist Menace at such a terrible cost in blood and lives.

Had it already been two years? The cold outside often burrowed deep into his bones in the morning. Especially today. Coffee might help.

And it might not, given the look on the General's face.

"What news, sir?" Gennadi asked, intent on meeting whatever it was that was coming.

Had the General Staff decided that he was washed up? Time to retire, even at forty-six? Or had he made some mistake somewhere and was about to be purged by one of Stalin's lackeys?

He'd watched it happen more than once as a young officer, only managing to escape by keeping his head down and working to be the best pilot in the Red Army Air Forces.

It had been enough to survive the Germans.

"Gennadi, I have a project," the General finally said heavily, after several false starts that saw coffee delivered and Yefim vanished again. "Some questioned me, but I have, for now, pushed back sufficiently that they will allow me to organize things as I see fit. It will be hard. It will be dangerous. It runs the risk that you will get crossways with certain kulaks in pretty uniforms that will grow jealous of you, but I honestly believe that you are the best man to handle it."

Gennadi let his surprise show. He hadn't expected that the General had that high an opinion of him. They had hardly spoken outside of official duties.

Apparently, he had impressed the man somewhere along the way.

"What does the Motherland need of me, Comrade General?" he asked soberly.

General Shuysky's Siberian face broke into a smile.

"Yes, Colonel," he said at some inside joke. "Yes. You do not ask what I need. Or what you can do. You rise above all of us and ask what the nation needs. *That* is why I chose you."

Gennadi nodded warily. He supposed that it was true. Rise to your excellence while not stepping on other faces as you go. Communism needed all men and women.

It was a dream that the world of the old czars and aristocracy could be swept away, allowing everyone freedom to become the artist locked somewhere in their soul.

"We have been tracking the war criminals, Colonel Nazarenko," the General continued. "There are always rumors that Hitler himself escaped us, but more than that, there is that rat bastard in the Vatican who loathes us with every fiber of his being. Probably because we come so much closer to living the dream of their prophet than those catamites in silk gowns will ever accomplish. That is neither here nor there. Austria has previously been hiding many of our targets. With various men like Roman Bishop Alois Hudal helping, the war criminals have been able to escape our wrath, either to places like Franco's Spain, or various nations in South America where they are taken it without question."

Gennadi nodded. The office of the Main Intelligence Directorate where he worked, the *Glavnoye Razvedyvatel'noye Upravleniye* or *GRU*, was dedicated to finding those war criminals and bringing them to justice. Gennadi himself didn't particularly care one way or the other about Jews or Roma, but he could be their avenging angel anyway.

Some evil could not be allowed to exist.

"How can I assist, Comrade General?" Gennadi asked, sitting more upright and damning his war injuries that prevented him from returning to the field to handle such tasks himself.

"Winston Churchill spoke of the *Sinews of Peace*, Colonel Nazarenko," Shuysky noted quietly. "1946. Missouri. *An Iron Curtain* separating us into two worlds. The Americans have taken up the cause as well, throwing away our old alliance, even as they have decided that communism is a greater threat than fascism. They no longer welcome our assistance in hunting the Nazi war criminals, possibly because they employ so many these days."

He paused there for a moment.

"It becomes necessary, then, to remove our fingerprints from the task."

Gennadi nodded, mostly as a placeholder, uncertain what the General Staff and the Party had come up with, but willing to hold the blade in his one, good hand for as long as he could.

Some evil could not be allowed to exist.

"You will create a special unit for the GRU, Colonel," General Shuysky said, handing Gennadi the folder. "It will operate in the West, in public, but its connection to the Soviet Union must remain entirely secret at all times. They will be a global force, operating well outside of our normal spheres of influence and reach, so they must be as self-sufficient as possible. At the same time, it is necessary to ensure their reliability, because they will be beset on all sides by the corruption and decadence of capitalism in its unbridled hunger. You yourself will be the only secure contact that they have, with secondary plans to reach me if something happens to you. This has been cleared and ordered at the very highest levels, Comrade Colonel. Read this summary."

The highest levels? Stalin himself had approved such a thing? *Ordered* it?

Gennadi felt a pang of fear trace icy fingers up his spine. At the same time, General Shuysky had selected him.

He read the document, noting that it was as top secret as could be arranged, with a short list of initials indicating everyone who had read it. He paused and added his sixth, at the bottom of the column.

Gennadi read the summary a second time, digesting the appalling scope of what the General Staff was ordering. The men he selected would become traitors to the Motherland, at least on paper. And probably in person. And yet, Comrade General Shuysky demanded patriots who could live such a double life for perhaps years, in order to get close enough to their targets to kill them, or at least destroy whatever cover identities they might have fled under?

"How much leeway do I have, Comrade General?" Gennadi asked when he finally looked up and felt the weight of history itself settle on his shoulders.

"As much as you need, Colonel Nazarenko," the man nodded darkly. "Perhaps enough rope to hang us both."

Yes, Gennadi could see that.

CHAPTER 5

Sasha looked up at the sound of boots approaching his cell. Concrete on five sides. Two-centimeter iron bars on the sixth. One metal bunk. One mattress just barely thick enough to count. One blanket that might be thicker than his uniform pants. Maybe.

The only light came from the hallway, a bare bulb not quite close enough to shine directly in, leaving most of his space in a cold, wet darkness that he knew would begin to gnaw on his soul in another few days.

Boots. Heavy, angry tread. Two sets. Two men.

Both appeared, dressed in the shoulder boards of the *Ministry of State Security*. The Secret Police.

A third man trailed them silently, limping some with the assistance of a cane. Dressed in the uniform of the Air Forces. A Colonel, no less.

The colonel came to rest as one of the guards indicated Sasha.

"Open the door, then return to your duty stations," the man ordered brusquely.

"But he is a prisoner, Comrade Colonel," the man protested.

"Unless you wish to be transferred to a volcano monitoring station in Kamchatka, you will do as I say," the man snarled quietly. "Am I clear?"

Both guards turned white. The one unlocked the iron door, then both fled as if the newcomer was chasing them with his cane as a cudgel.

Sasha remained seated on his bunk, watching as the man moved just out of sight, then drew a wooden chair with him as he entered Sasha's cell.

The older man sat and settled, his cane leaning against the bars.

"Major Kryvenko, I am Colonel Gennadi Nazarenko of the GRU," the man said in a weary tone.

Sasha watched him with emotionless eyes. Presumably, someone had grown jealous and filed a report with some secret police informer, intending that Sasha be destroyed for whatever petty reasons men like that chose.

He had seen it happen all too often.

"I was the one who ordered you arrested," Nazarenko continued. "I have been reviewing your files and I have a mission that I believe you would be exceptionally well suited to undertaking."

"A mission, Comrade Colonel?" Sasha finally asked, trying to keep the disdain out of his voice.

Who did this man think he was?

"You were never allowed to be a hero during the Great Patriotic War, Major," the man nodded. "Instead, you accepted whatever mission or business you were assigned and did it with calm dignity and superior focus. Perhaps you should have been on the front, but it was more important making sure that the front did not collapse. You helped that."

Sasha nodded warily. As good a description as any. Jobs that needed doing, because the pilots needed aircraft, at a time when only the Americans and British could build fast enough. Or training the children who might go out and never return on their first mission.

He had sent too many of them to their deaths, but everyone had understood that the only way to destroy the Nazi Menace had involved drowning it in Slavic blood.

Far too much blood.

"You are a quiet patriot, Major Kryvenko," Nazarenko nodded. "A reliable soldier who is still capable of greatness, when he is not leashed to the confines of smaller minds."

Sasha couldn't help the jolt of surprise that flowed through him.

The Colonel smiled.

"Yes," he nodded. "People noticed. Until now, we could not make use of such a thing. That has changed."

"Colonel?" Sasha asked, sliding over into a hint of bewilderment now.

"Far too many Germans escaped us in '45, Major," Nazarenko continued. "I have been part of a small, hidden organization inside the GRU dedicated to hunting them down, regardless of where they go. Too many think that they can flee justice. They may be correct in that, because global revolution will take time to take root. Time to grow the bitter fruit that is the legacy of colonialism. Time to poison the capitalists and see them dead. We no longer have that luxury."

Sasha heard the rage under the words. Noted that the man's injuries might be from the war. That Nazarenko might be broken in body, but his soul was still fire.

"Colonel, why am I here?" Sasha finally asked.

"Because I need to break you, Major Kryvenko," the man said soberly. "Cast you out of the home you have known, and do so publicly so that others might believe it. I need you to become an agent, Sasha Kryvenko. My agent. My avenging angel to hunt down the fascists in places where the Party and the Revolution may not follow."

Sasha heard the words, but didn't process them. Nazarenko nodded.

"I need a weapon, Sasha," he continued. "I need a public trial and conviction. I need you to make a daring escape to the West, where you will be provided a cover that lets you get close enough to stop them. Any fool might do, but High Command demands a patriot who is willing to accept a terrible duty and the horrible scorn that will come with it. Because it might be years before you can return to the fold, though we will know the truth. Sasha, I need a hero."

Sasha let the tones flow over him. The rage. The fire. The many ugly things that the Germans had undertaken in the name of their *Lebensraum*. Their Living Space, to be carved from the soul of the Soviet Motherland.

Silence fell.

Stretched.

Filled the hollow concrete box that had been his life for the last day.

"What do I need to do, Comrade Colonel?" Sasha asked.

CHAPTER 6

Gennadi nodded.

It was a terrible thing he was doing to the man. Nothing less than evil itself would have compelled him, but the need was that great.

Some evil could not be allowed to exist.

"I cannot ask you to trust me, Major," he told the man. "Not yet. That will come later, when you are found guilty of treason and sentenced to death."

"Why me?" Kryvenko asked. "What was the one thing that selected me? Surely you must have had others."

Gennadi was most impressed by how calmly the man seemed to be taking all this, but it might also be the shock not yet worn off.

"I did," Gennadi nodded. "A few. You would be surprised how many I disqualified because I knew that they would eventually fall victim to that siren call of Westernism. But a few I could pass. All of you pilots. Single men who spoke English and other languages, and had the ability to learn more easily. What selected you above them, Sasha Kryvenko? You are a killer, when you need to be. And a man who can turn it off when it is not appropriate. Too many see violence as the best solution. It is always one solution, but many times there will be better ones you can employ. I needed both a solid thinker and a man of action. Later, you will lead a team, but right now I need to get you into the field to track down a series of rumors."

"Of?" Kryvenko pressed.

Gennadi held up his mostly useless left arm. He could lift a fork with it. Hold a knife. On a good day, lift a mug of coffee or tea.

Not much more.

"In April of 1945, we were closing in on Berlin," Gennadi began, flashing back to the pain that always came when he remembered. "The Germans had been driven back from Leningrad. From Stalingrad. From Moscow. Kursk had broken their momentum and their teeth and they were dying, but not fast enough. I was a pilot like you, flying a Lavochkin La-7 on that day. A hundred aircraft met in the skies over Berlin and fought, but it came down to a singular duel for me. My foe was a German captain named Alois Voss, flying a Focke-Wulf Ta 152. We dueled for half an hour, before a final pass left us both destroyed. I managed to limp far enough that a Guards Tank unit rescued me when I crashed, though not without harm. I had thought Voss dead. Until now."

"Until now?" Sasha perked up.

"Our new embassy in Argentina has reported a sighting of the man two months ago," Gennadi replied. "Worse, he appears to be designing some new aircraft. Something experimental, using stolen plans he paid American spies to acquire for him. Also, he is in hiding while doing so, and not working with the Americans or the Argentinians, as many of his contemporaries are. I need you to find out why. What he is doing. And how we can stop him."

Sasha nodded, obviously still deep in thought, but not immediately hostile. Or fallen into a terrible depression.

Steeling himself.

"Can one man really make a difference, Comrade Colonel?" Sasha asked quietly, underlining all the reasons Gennadi had disqualified so many others.

"One man can," Gennadi assured him. "But he will not be alone for long. While you are seeking, I intend to locate others that can be added to a team you will command. If they can learn quickly enough, they may travel with you, but I need you in South America as soon as possible. Will you be my weapon of justice, Sasha?"

The man seemed to shrink in on himself for a long moment, then a breath inflated him. Head up. Eyes stern. Fists flexed once into fists, then relaxed.

"I will do what I can, Comrade Colonel," he said.

"That, Sasha, is all any of us can do," Gennadi replied. "And all I can ask."

CHAPTER 7

Sasha kept his temper in check as the guards manacled him and thrust him roughly before them, occasionally bouncing him off walls and corners while taunting him with cruel voices.

The Colonel had warned that he could tell no one of what was coming. That Sasha would have to face this portion entirely alone, building the legend that would serve him later.

Whatever was coming.

He was driven like a bull into a small room. Waist-high platform with three people seated behind a table, above and looking down. Sasha was delivered to a small table below and in front, where his two guards pushed him down and loomed over each shoulder.

"Major Aleksandr Kryvenko, you have been accused of treason to the Motherland," the man in the middle began without prologue.

That one wore no uniform, unlike the two unknown Air Forces colonels that flanked him. Wire rim glasses. Slicked hair. Weasel face.

State Security. Necessary during revolutionary times, but now simply a shiv and a maul designed to crush any opposition to the party. Any resistance.

Anyone.

Sasha waited.

"Have you nothing to say for yourself?" the man sneered.

"I am a loyal soldier, comrade," Sasha replied. "Dedicated to the Party and the eventual liberation of the world from evil."

More sneers. Even the colonels joined him, though slowly and cringing, as if aware that they might be next on the chopping block.

Sasha wondered if a new purge was slowly gathering steam. Stalin was old and many might be maneuvering to replace him when he went.

The man began reading a list of charges that was itself rather impressive. Corruption. Theft. Espionage. Even a third of it might be enough to be executed as a traitor. They were making a point with him.

And all he had to go on was Colonel Nazarenko's word. Still, it gave him strength.

"How do you plead?"

"All of those are lies and fabrications," Sasha replied evenly. "Fables invented to remove a loyal party member that others who crave his place might take it."

"Enough," the man in the middle snarled. "You may plead for mercy from the court and admit everything, or be sentenced to death. Which will it be?"

"I will die with honor," Sasha replied coldly.

"So be it," the man nodded. A hand found a gavel and rapped it once. "Guards, return the prisoner to his cell while we fill out and sign his execution warrant."

Sasha was dragged upright from a chair he hadn't even sat in long enough to warm. Hands clamped on his elbows and he was removed.

The walls closed in quickly once they left him alone. Wet concrete cold and dim, with only the one light down the hall providing any illumination.

Sasha sat on the edge of the bed and waited, wondering if his desperate imagination had created Colonel Nazarenko as a defense against madness.

No sound intruded, but Sasha turned to his right and the Colonel was standing there, having somehow silently arrived.

Sasha rose to his feet.

"Are you ready, Sasha?" the man asked. "I cannot call you Major anymore, because that is being stripped even as we speak. Now, you will escape and become a fugitive."

PART TWO

FLIGHT

CHAPTER 8

Sasha could remember every step along the path, but it still seemed a bizarre dream he would awaken from at any moment, back in that cold, dank cell, sleeping in the shadow of the hangman's noose.

Out of the cell and down a long series of service tunnels before emerging briefly in the boiler room and being chivied onto a loading dock and into the back of a truck, Colonel Nazarenko somehow keeping up in spite of a cane. A drive down pitted roads in an old Zis that needed a new clutch and should have had the carburetor adjusted for the cold weather.

An hour of bone-chilling arctic air because all he had was his uniform and a great coat someone had thrown on his shoulders, occasionally spying snow when the tarp over the truck flapped. Silence but for the sounds of the road.

Then an airport. Dark and seemingly abandoned, so he had wondered if it had been dropped from use after the war and ignored, save for the large jet aircraft parked at one end of the runway when the truck stopped.

Sasha's surprise at the pilot, his old transport comrade, Senior Lieutenant Yuri Datsyuk, who had gone on to train pilots in the IL-2 *Sturmovik* during the war when Sasha had taught the fighter pilots.

The craft itself, a camouflaged prototype he recognized from Ilyushin, their new medium bomber, modified until it was nearly impossible to identify, even when he'd previously flown the beast.

Then more flight, this time actual flight. Poland, to another air strip with nothing lit but the runway and the fuel truck parked at one end.

Dawn had chased them down over the North Sea, pretending to be a private cargo carrier headed to Ireland, but they had still skirted the southern flanks of England, before landing outside Dublin, only a generation escaped from the imperialists.

Sleep for a time, then lunch, where an ununiformed man silently escorted Sasha to a commissary and turned him over to Yuri again.

"What is this place?" Sasha asked over better coffee than he expected. And sweet rolls.

"The Irish would reclaim the rest of their island from the English," Yuri replied in crisp English, so Sasha switched languages automatically to follow. "They are friends with the Party, but it is more of a fellow travelers thing than ideological compatibility."

"Freedom from oppression, yes," Sasha acknowledged.

The Irish had largely stayed neutral during the war against the Germans. Not that they had had any great love of fascism, but because they had **centuries** of anger at England.

"And our place?" Sasha said after a bite and sip.

"Imagine my surprise when I was approached about defecting," Yuri grinned. "Only when I learned who it was that was involved did I come to understand that there was something much deeper involved. Colonel Nazarenko briefed me that you were on a special, long-term, undercover mission, and recruited me to join you. And put *Verblyud* at your service to fly you around."

The Ilyushin Camel. Sasha nodded. It had indeed been a useful pack animal, though he would need more at some point. Jet fighters, which the Colonel had also promised were coming, but time was key right now. Sasha had to get to South America to investigate the rumors, and couldn't wait weeks for a ship.

It was a pity that no jet aircraft currently had the range and the speed, though he knew it was only a matter of time. Only old bombers from the war.

Time was what he didn't have.

"What has the Colonel told you?" Sasha asked, glancing around and realizing that there was nobody in sight, in spite of how large the room was.

Even the kitchen staff had gotten them food, then closed the hatch separating rooms.

"Fascists in hiding," Yuri said. "Unable to be hunted publicly because the British and Americans no longer see the Soviet Union as allies, but as a threat that must be *Contained*. Possibly destroyed."

"And we must play the role of traitors to the Motherland that have escaped," Sasha nodded. "Mercenaries for hire. Trained pilots and soldiers. Later, he promised me a team, but for now, it is just the two of us."

"As it was in Persia, my old friend," Yuri smiled. "And later. Have you recovered enough to continue?"

"I believe so," Sasha nodded.

He was unprepared for Yuri to put two fingers in his mouth and whistle loudly. That same soldier appeared a few moments later, studied them, and nodded.

"This way," he said in an English painted over with a hard Irish lilt.

Sasha and Yuri rose and followed him out into daylight that had been hidden by closed shutters. The day was cool but not as bitter as Moscow had been. Or Poland.

Then ended up in a small hut, with a letter from the Colonel atop a trunk.

Sasha tore it open and read orders. Requests, really, in the form of a personal letter that hinted at things not obvious to anyone else reading it. New flying gear to exchange for the old stuff. Various equipment they might need on their journey. The usual.

Yuri had opened the trunk the letter had been resting on and pulled out a new jacket. Sasha was tall and lean for a Soviet pilot. One hundred and eighty-five centimeters tall and seventy-eight kilograms. The two uniforms were obvious, as Yuri was both taller and broader.

They changed from the dark blue of Soviet aviation, with pullover tunics and poofy jodhpurs into more form-fitting pants of a brighter blue, matched by a T-shirt/overshirt combination worn under a medium blue jacket that buttoned up the right side like an overdone double-breasted suit with a black leather belt.

Much more durable, and they kept the black leather calf boots with the good walking tread.

Instead of the previous pilotka cap, with the Soviet star on the brow, these had a kite shield logo on the left side, a red Stag head on sky blue, with horns up both sides and a globe between the antlers, showing the Atlantic Ocean bounded on both sides.

"We are now called the Red Branch," Sasha announced, checking the details the Colonel had left at the bottom of the note, just above the instructions to burn the letter after reading.

"A fitting name, given our location," Yuri smiled.

Then he pulled out a pair of small boxes, not much larger than cigar sized.

Inside, a matched pair of pistols. At first glance, Mauser C96 Broomhandle, but Sasha saw the Chinese writing on the side and understood. Much larger. Shanxi Type 17. Chinese made by a warlord there during the last generation. Rechambered to the American .45 ACP. In this case, rebuilt with removable magazines holding twenty rounds, such that they extended almost as far down as the handle.

Two of them, with cleaning kits, spare magazines, and ammunition. Resting atop a pair of American Thompson submachine guns, furthering their legend as being Russians who had escaped

Soviet control and were somehow being funded and supported by some Western *someone* that would remain elusive.

He and Yuri were spies, intended to operate somewhat in the open, in perhaps the most dangerous game possible. Every bit of camouflage would help.

They left their old clothing and gear behind, gathering up the trunk and carrying it outside, where that same soldier nodded to two others that had appeared. Those two, utterly silent, carried the trunk to the jet and loaded it, while the soldier escorted them, handing them another sealed packet then turning and walking away without another word.

Sasha joined Yuri in the aircraft, taking the forward position for the Navigator/Bombardier. They had no tail gunner to operate the radio, but also didn't have anyone to talk to save various flight control towers along the way, so that was fine.

The packet was more orders. Or rather, a series of destinations where they could land, refuel, and continue, sleeping occasionally while local mechanics would handle prearranged maintenance. Galway, on the western edge of Ireland, where they would pick up external fuel tanks that would get them to Red Point, Newfoundland. To Mount Pleasant, Michigan. To Havana, Cuba. To Quito, Ecuador. To La Paz, Bolivia. Finally to Buenos Aires, Argentina.

Where the chase would turn quite serious.

Sasha began plotting his flight vectors as Yuri got them rolling down the runway.

He had a man to find in South America.

CHAPTER 9

Sasha looked around the hotel's bar and noted that it was a broad mix of what looked like international businessmen and criminals from the ways they warily eyed one another.

He had been running for weeks at this point. Had he only been arrested three months ago? It felt like a lifetime. Like he had stepped into a forest clearing and the Baba Yaga had catapulted him through a portal into a magical realm.

It didn't help that they were in the southern hemisphere, where the day was much warmer than Moscow had been. Late summer now, though a mild, Mediterranean one.

He was now a spy. Of sorts. Living a double life, as he began stalking his prey, using whatever means he could, as long as he remained hidden in his role.

Yuri did not trust the locals all that much, so had elected to stay at the small airport where they had stashed their camel, in spite of instructions that the people running the place were largely covert operatives. Locals hired and vetted by the Party.

Peron had a long history of hating the Party and welcoming various fascists once the European war crushed their dreams of world domination and *Lebensraum.* Living space, acquired by conquering and exterminating the Slavs.

Sasha had a few opinions on the topic, but this newly escaped and defected version of him had to pretend to be a capitalist stooge. An imperialist. Shadowy trails would eventually—one hoped—dead end in Ireland with the founding of a new mercenary company called *Red Branch*.

For now, he had taken a room at the same hotel where William Jacobs had been murdered. The trail was cold after this long, but it was a starting point.

Sasha had never been to South America. Had never been west of Berlin or south of Tehran, for all he had flown. The Soviet Union itself was vast, and his lifetime had seen massive changes.

He had been born in Imperial Russia. Lived through a revolution and civil war. Survived the hard years and the purges. Fought in the Great Patriotic War.

Now he was hunting the evil that had been allowed to escape, rather than face their justice at places like Nuremberg. Or Siberia.

The funniest part, at least to Sasha, was how much Peron had pursued socialist tendencies before coming to power, intending to build up Argentina into a major international power while not being beholden to the United States or the Soviet Union. Had the Americans left him alone, he might have even been their ally, but Washington saw everything in black and white, while places like Argentina ran the entire spectrum of grays, with nobody loudly announcing their loyalties because people were purged and rehabilitated so often. Even Peron had faced such things, so Sasha assumed that the man's willingness to shelter Nazis was more to get back at the Americans than anything.

That, and import so much technical expertise from people unwilling to embrace modern socialism.

Sasha shrugged in his head as a man entered. Why the figure stood out, Sasha could not say, but he did. Civilian attire, but he moved as if the brown suit felt alien.

That was it. A man used to a uniform, adjusting to being out of it. Like Sasha, though his new costume was much closer.

Hiding, by not hiding, as the Colonel had suggested.

The man spied Sasha at his table and carefully made his way

closer. Middle age. Slicked back hair that looked black. Swarthy in the way of Iberians rather than Slavs. A bit jowly and paunchy, but not badly out of shape.

Ex-military, perhaps, but not a former pilot. He didn't have that look about him.

And he came to rest at a polite distance, back ramrod straight and almost looking like he had to stop himself from clicking his heels.

"Major Kryvenko?" he asked.

"Major no more," Sasha replied. "I left that behind me when I escaped."

The man nodded at some internal monologue and indicated the chair across the table.

That he knew Sasha had been a major previously meant that the man was associated with the government. Or A government. A spy or a secret policeman of some sort.

For whom?

"May I?" the man asked.

Sasha nodded, then watched the stranger sit, snapping his fingers at a nearby waiter for more wine. Obviously, known around here, as a bottle arrived quickly, got opened, and poured before the waiter withdrew.

"Felix Melendez," he introduced himself and they shook hands. "A certain somebody suggested that I look you up."

Sasha nodded. From this moment forward, his entire life would be a lie, because he had no way to prove who this new person he was might be, had gone so far away that the Colonel could not help him in South America.

"I am hoping to be safe here while I sort out my options," Sasha replied.

"How did you come to be here?" Melendez asked. "I appreciate that you claim to have escaped the Soviet Union, but why Argentina?"

"Western Europe is not safe for me," Sasha replied. "The Whites that escaped the Revolution might live in Paris, but I have heard stories about many of them being disappeared off the streets by Soviet agents. The Americans would treat me like the people I fled, or demand that I become a double agent for them and go back to my certain doom. Argentina seeks its Third Way, and I hope in that place that I can find someone willing to employ me."

All truth, just shaded. And what a man newly fled to Buenos Aires might say to someone he expected to be a government official, however *sub rosa*.

"Then it's true that you broke out of a Soviet prison one step ahead of a death sentence?" Melendez asked.

Sasha shrugged.

"I had friends who were able to smuggle me out, at the risk of their own lives," he offered. "One accompanied me this far, an old comrade from the war who wasn't willing to watch his friends be tortured and killed."

"And what did you do before?" Melendez pressed, eyes narrow as he sipped his wine.

Sasha assumed that someone, somewhere, had leaked the official reports. That they knew most of his answers before he gave them.

At least the cover story.

How well would it hold up? How soon would someone try to kill him, either a fascist settling old scores or a loyal comrade believing the lies?

How did one live in such a hall of twisted mirrors?

"I most recently worked with several design bureaus around Moscow as a test pilot and consultant," Sasha nodded. "The skills that flew many different kinds of aircraft during the war are not necessarily the same when things are jet powered, but my flexibility was a benefit. And nobody truly understands how the machines will operate, so the designers need pilots close to answer questions and fly experimental aircraft that might not be ready to develop more fully."

"And you were purged?" Melendez seemingly pounced on that word.

"I was arrested," Sasha corrected him. "The charges were a fantabulist's dream, none of which had any bearing on reality. When they signed my death warrant, friends smuggled me out and got me to Poland, where others got me eventually to Ireland. There, I was given funds by some industrialists that thought I might be able to find mercenary employment in South America, because the Irish share a deep and abiding loathing of the British and Americans for how they were treated during the past. Past that, I haven't been here long enough to do more than meet with a few folks and answer some questions. Were you from the government, or perhaps someone looking to hire a pilot?"

He narrowed down on the man. Was he about to be arrested? Deported? Shot? Recruited?

Nobody had been able to offer any hint as to what might happen when this moment arrived.

Only that his next mistake would likely be his last.

CHAPTER 10

Sasha wished that his cover identity allowed him to be armed, but it did not. And the crossover jacket he wore precluded a shoulder holster of any kind. The best he could eventually do might be a pocket pistol, possibly in a belt pouch. Assuming he wasn't in a place where a holster on his belt was appropriate.

"Are you familiar with the Horton Brothers?" Melendez asked obliquely.

"German aircraft designers before and during the war," Sasha nodded, pausing to take a sip as if remembering. The new wine was pretty good. "Research on flying wing designs, though I don't remember if any of them ever made it to production."

"Correct on both accounts," Melendez nodded back. "And a third brother killed early in the war. One of them lives not that far from here and continues his research for new kinds of civilian aircraft that should have tremendous range."

Sasha pretended surprise at those words. The Colonel had told him Horton and Northrop had both been pushing the envelope with such things, and presumed that Alois Voss—the Blue Wolf himself—had far too much interest in such things, based on the man he had killed.

Then Sasha nodded, as if satisfied. Many Germans had fled

Europe. Not all of them were evil that needed to be expunged. Some had merely served, instead of fighting on the front lines.

Like Sasha, for most of the war.

"Is he building planes?" Sasha asked.

"Designing them, if nothing else," Melendez replied. "The government was interested if he had contacted you."

"I didn't even know he was here," Sasha said. "Or which brother, since you mentioned only one. I suppose he might wish to hire me when he needed a test pilot. Or others, needing such skills. What is the government up to along those lines? Or civilian aviation? I've not had much luck finding people who might be interested in employing me."

"But you are available?" Melendez pursued.

"Indeed," Sasha nodded, wondering whether he was about to be arrested or hired.

So much hinged on the next words out of this man's mouth.

"You mentioned mercenary work earlier?" Melendez hesitated.

Sasha merely nodded, glancing about.

Nobody else in the room stood out. Nor were any of the men in here paying any great attention to this conversation, so he didn't think more secret police were about to pounce on him.

At least he hoped not.

"I represent a group of industrialists, Major Kryvenko." Melendez turned a bit formal, though his voice dropped to almost nothing. "We might be interested in hiring you as a mercenary pilot, at least for a few short-term missions, if you were interested?"

"Is the pay good?" Sasha asked.

Colonel Nazarenko had mentioned that to be the single most important question to most mercenaries. Not the politics of the employer or target. Merely the pay.

"It is, Major," Melendez said with a smile. "How well do you know the US Republic P-47 Thunderbolt?"

"Interceptor and ground-attack aircraft," Sasha nodded. "The

Soviet Union used them extensively during the war. I've flown in them, but mostly to train other pilots."

"They are fairly common in Latin America these days, Major," Melendez continued. "We'd like to hire you to pilot one. A test mission, if you will, before perhaps extending a more permanent employment contract."

"Is it well maintained?" Sasha pushed back. "Properly serviced, up to date, all of that? It is a lovely aircraft, but can be finicky if the mechanics get lazy."

"I can introduce you to the men working on the craft," Melendez nodded. "It is in private service at present, but the men are all formerly of the Air Services."

Sasha studied the man closer, as if reading his honesty.

For now, any job would do, because he needed to establish his credentials with the locals.

"Should we retire someplace more private to go deeper into the details?" Sasha asked.

Melendez studied him back, then nodded.

"Yes," the man said, rising. "I believe that would be a wise choice."

Sasha rose as well, towering somewhat over the smaller man, but leaning back a bit so as to not emphasize it.

Whatever *it* was, it had begun.

CHAPTER 11

Sasha felt that he had driven a pretty good bargain, in spite of being both desperate to work and not really needing the cash.

Still, it had gotten him here, though he wasn't entirely certain where he was.

As with the flight from the prison, he'd been taken at night through Buenos Aires streets and then various rural landscapes, eventually arriving at an airport. He thought that they had gone well beyond Rosario, along the Paraná River, but it had been dark and they had driven for much of the night, though the highway had been pleasant and there had been many towns along the way.

This morning, a small airstrip seemingly cut out of the jungle. Sasha wondered how much of his life forward might be measured by such things.

Food hot and fresh by several women who never smiled. Armed guards but none of them wearing uniforms. Two Thunderbolts in a hangar that he'd been allowed to see. Mechanics hard at work on the nearer one, including adding a number of bombs under the wings. Small ones, but obvious.

He was sipping coffee with Melendez in the canteen, while two men watched from nearby, silent and probably intimidating in their own heads.

Sasha wasn't all that impressed by them. He turned back to

Melendez, apparently his controller, since this was being run like some sort of espionage operation.

He wondered who was providing the money and official support, but doubted that these were the people he was intending to infiltrate.

At least so far. Colonel Nazarenko would probably appreciate some future report, but Sasha had to memorize things for now.

"What can you tell me?" Sasha asked blandly.

"Tomorrow morning, you will fly a bombing mission," Melendez smiled cruelly.

Sasha shrugged.

"I saw the one aircraft being readied," he countered. "Is the other flyable? I would appreciate being able to refresh myself on the Thunderbolt if it was. Even thirty minutes or an hour in the air would be quite helpful in making sure I had everything in memory."

Melendez scowled, eyes narrowing.

"Where would you go?" he demanded.

"I'm not even certain where I am," Sasha reminded him. "Presumably, the mission briefing will have that information. I have been flying experimental jet aircraft more recently, and the flight characteristics are radically different from propellers and pistons. This is making sure I'm ready, presumably to bomb and strafe some target you want eliminated anonymously."

Because while the two aircraft had been obvious, both had been painted underneath with a faded blue that would be harder to spot from the ground, while the tops had been a nice forest green, also invisible against forests below.

At least if you didn't have radar keeping watch, and he doubted that the Siberian backwoods of South America would.

Melendez seemed surprised, but got over himself quickly.

"Yes, I forget that you are smarter than most mercenaries," he nodded. "While you sleep, I will contact my superiors and inquire."

Sasha nodded.

They were paying him to kill people. That's what mercenaries did, when you stripped away all the patriotism and emotional loading.

Kill people.

And his mission called for that, in order to sustain his cover.

So be it.

CHAPTER 12

Sasha had enjoyed an hour of test flying yesterday, remembering the Thunderbolts he had trained and tested during the war. Not much had changed, save that it was slower and the engines growled at a lower tone than jets.

The airstrip had ended up being north of Santa Fe, but he only knew that because he'd had the maps. His target today was across the river in Uruguay, driving south on the highway from Salto and supposedly obvious when seen from above.

Two trucks and a staff car escorting them. Sasha hadn't asked who they were, or why Melendez and his superiors wanted them dead. Merely confirmed that he had four two-hundred pound bombs attached, a full load of ammunition for the eight M2 machine guns, and that the flight characteristics of the aircraft were good.

Utterly flawless day for flying. No clouds anywhere on the horizon. Visibility seemingly forever.

Sasha missed having a wingman to protect him, but in many ways, the radio silence took him back to the early days of the war, when many aircraft lacked radios entirely.

He was a knight-errant on a quest. Evil quest, or perhaps questionable deeds in service of something better. Nothing that would stain his soul, because he had a greater mission and this was merely a step in that direction.

He was flying fairly high, to the point that the highway was a gray river with black dots on it. The trucks would eventually arrive at Montevideo, if he failed.

Sasha didn't intend to fail.

Circling from the north, he lined up the road and dialed back the throttle until things started to grow sluggish as he approached stall speed. He had the timing when the convoy supposedly had left Salto, and the highway turned from south to southwest about two-thirds of the way to Paysandú, before turning and running straight southeast once past.

He'd taken off at first light, slipping across the river into what he supposed might be an act of war if he was shot down or crashed, though Sasha doubted that the situation was anything more than rival gangs of businessmen as criminals.

The Colonel had warned him that he was about to enter a world of gangsters.

There. Two green trucks. The American Deuce-and-a-Half that had been so common, supplied by seemingly endless American factories as a flatbed transport to stop the Nazis.

Ahead of them, an open-topped Mercedes staff car like the Germans had used. He wondered if it was surplus, or stolen. Or simply carried off by Germans fleeing.

Sasha shrugged and banked away, still far too high to do anything precise.

Instead, he tipped the nose over and accelerated. Paysandú was visible some ten miles in the distance. He needed to finish them off now, before they could somehow find cover in the city.

Assuming that he wouldn't drop bombs on civilians.

Sasha hadn't confronted the edges of his legend yet. Hopefully, that wasn't going to happen today, either.

Circling, he lined himself up on the highway again, understanding that most people would merely see him as a barnstorming pilot.

At least until he opened fire. That was coming.

Two trucks, maintaining a reasonable driving distance, without much traffic around them. Straight road without much cover to either side as this was mostly farm country and they'd already crossed the bridge where the highway slowed everything down.

He didn't need to cut a road or bridge to prevent reinforcements from arriving, either.

Merely kill people.

Sasha lined up his sights and triggered the cannons, letting the aircraft be slowed by the tremendous recoil of eight 12.7mm guns, the ubiquitous American M2 Fifty.

The burst struck the rear truck like a sledgehammer. Sasha pulled back on his stick enough to bring his nose up as he triggered a second burst into the front truck.

Below, havoc as war suddenly descended on a quiet highway. War that most of South America had largely avoided.

The front truck began smoking as he blasted past. Engine or fuel fires threatening. Sasha pulled up and rolled onto one wing to survey his effort.

The trucks were both stopped, with the front one possibly about to explode. The staff car had continued on, but was slowing. Other vehicles in sight were speeding up or slowing down as their drivers saw fit or panicked

Sasha got more distance and snapped a tight turn back. This time, men had spilled out of the vehicles and seemed to be shooting back at him, though with pistols and submachine guns that were more security blanket than threat.

Still, it made him feel better that they were prepared for violence, instead of being a church group on a trip. Not that he had much use for the Christian God, but it seemed to bring comfort to some. Or was a useful tool to control an otherwise restive population.

Sasha split his mind, sighting the two trucks with one eye and the staff car with the other. Yuri had spoken of such techniques, back when they had been trainers, so he was familiar with it.

And it helped that there were no heavy weapons or enemy aircraft.

Right?

Sasha fired a burst into the car, but paused and looked up in all directions, just in case he was about to be jumped by Nazis.

Nothing.

And he'd overshot his target.

Good enough.

This time, he rolled left and came around. The staff car was abandoned, so he presumed the passengers had either died or more likely fled to the ditch to hide.

His target was the pair of trucks anyway.

Sasha slowed and practically glided in, dropping his first two bombs and quickly pulling up and away while slamming on the throttle to gain altitude and speed.

A pair of brilliant, yellow eggs when he glanced back, engulfing the trucks in a maelstrom of hot fury.

Sasha nodded, then circled away. He was being paid for professionalism. Today, that involved the other two bombs on his next run, dropped low and slow, plus about half of his ammunition.

He would retain the other half in case someone did scramble air defenses and vector them down on him. Sasha wouldn't assume amateur pilots, but he knew himself to be among the best the Red Air Force had, which should be among the best in the world.

Circling back, he began his next attack run.

CHAPTER 13

Sasha feathered the propeller blades as he came to rest, not far from his hangar.

He preferred jets, but the old Thunderbolt had served well in the war. And had flown quite perfectly today, leaving a flaming mess and several dead bodies on a highway in Uruguay.

Shutting everything down, he opened his canopy, unbuckled, and rose. The ground crew was already in motion, and would service everything, so he removed his helmet and hopped down.

A car arrived as he got settled. The door opened and Melendez waved him in.

Sasha took a deep breath and consigned his soul to whatever was going to happen next.

"Successful, Major?" Melendez asked as Sasha got settled and they drove off.

"Both trucks destroyed," Sasha nodded. "The staff car was on fire when I left, because I'd put all four bombs into the trucks. I presume you'll be able to pull the gun cameras and review, but the worst that might happen is that some of the men in the vehicles survived."

The man nodded.

"And you, Major?" he pressed. "Did it feel good to be back in battle?"

Sasha shrugged.

"Not really fair, taking a Thunderbolt against civilian vehoc-less unprepared for me," he replied. "Although next time they might have some sort of air defense, either a heavy machine gun in a defensive turret or they might seek to hire their own aircraft to fly patrol cover. That would make it more like my time over Berlin. This was more of a training exercise, with some trainer keeping score on neatness and efficiency. I think he would score me pretty well."

They lapsed into silence. Sasha noted that they had already turned away from the main building and seemed to be leaving the small base, so presumably his mission was done.

Where were they taking him next?

Returning him to Buenos Aires? Or arresting him? Or shooting him to eliminate all witnesses to the crime?

Next time he had a chance, he would find and carry a small pistol that he could secrete about his gear. For now, he simply had to trust that they needed a skilled pilot and killer.

The great wars had largely ignored Latin America, with everyone maintaining some level of studied neutrality, save for occasional units of men raised to fight for the American army. Sasha doubted that there would be many expert combat pilots to be hired.

And, of course, Alois Voss was hiding somewhere.

"We have looked into the Red Branch, Major," Melendez suddenly broke the silence. "There is not much available."

Sasha nodded and tried to control his breathing and his pulse.

How deep had they looked? He had been assured that the covers set up would stop even the British and the Americans from learning the truth, but there were spies and double agents everywhere.

"Friends saw me as perhaps the first of a river of such victims," he lied smoothly. "That they expected another purge impending and otherwise loyal officers were going to be arrested and sent to die in work camps. Or executed for whatever charges the authorities think might stick. I can never return home. And will have to live the rest of my life looking over a shoulder for Soviet agents come to assassinate me."

"Is there any more to the Red Branch than you and Datsyuk?" Melendez asked.

So, the man and his superiors had dug in. And hopefully run into the wall erected to keep them out.

"Not yet," Sasha nodded. "This trip to Latin America was to see if there was a demand for experts such as myself in the mercenary field. If there is, then I will return to Ireland and see about recruiting more pilots and warriors though my contacts there. At some point, the colonial powers will be losing their overseas territories, either by letting them go or facing armed revolution. When you reach that stage of social development, it is usually not enough to merely buy guns, if you don't have experts using them. Similarly, such places will not have an available air corps that can help, so they will be looking to hire them."

"What about Soviet infiltration?" Melendez leaned in, eyes like a hawk's. "Communist agitation and revolution?"

"Trotsky is dead," Sasha replied. "Mexico City. 1940. His was the internationalist push. Stalin, as far as I know, defends the Motherland. Or you know more than I do."

"Would you fly against your old comrades?" Melendez asked.

"Is the pay good?" Sasha countered sharply. Always, always, always the mercenary. "They would kill me without hesitation. I would have none fighting them. Here, though, aren't you more likely to be facing American troops, intending to overthrow your government? That seems to be the entire *raison d'être* of the US Marine Corps."

Melendez fell silent, watching. Possibly re-calibrating, from the look on his face.

"We are traveling to meet someone, Major," Melendez began, but Sasha cut him off.

"Major no more," Sasha corrected him, letting his tone get a little stiff-necked and aggrieved. "I am Sasha Kryvenko at present.

Señor Kryvenko, I suppose. Major Kryvenko was sentenced to death and must largely vanish if I am to survive. I have even considered taking up some other *nom de guerre*, but am loathe to give up who I am."

"Señor Kryvenko, then," Melendez relented. "We travel to meet someone that might be interested in both hiring you, and perhaps hiring a larger unit, if you were able to turn your Red Branch into a fighting force. There are whispers that such a thing might be needed in the near future."

Sasha perked up, but Melendez lapsed into silence with a knowing smile.

Sasha did the same, watching the scenery pass.

Perhaps, he had made it past his first test.

How many more would there be?

CHAPTER 14

Palace.

Sasha supposed that the term *hacienda* was more appropriate, but the building was simply huge. White stone, roughly dressed, running four stories tall and seemingly forever in both directions from a front porch where heads of state could give speeches to large mobs.

The car came to rest with a squeak and Sasha followed Melendez out and up the steps to where a butler already held the enormous double door open.

Sasha felt badly out of place in his flying leathers, especially with the front unbuckled so he didn't overheat. The butler took a look and led him to a small mud room.

"You may leave your gear here," the man announced in a stiff, Teutonic accent, before withdrawing.

Sasha did, stripping back down to the blue that had become his signature color and costume. The pilotka hat stayed in a pocket, but the same logo was on his left shoulder.

They were led into a library that had the appearance of great age and wealth, but none of the homeyness of use. It felt more like a Potemkin village. Or a movie set.

Leather chairs that appeared to have been regularly dusted and almost never used. Books frequently behind glass fronts.

Tables where one might study while sitting in uncomfortable-looking chairs. Art objects of various flavors, dominated by four suits of European plate armor kept polished almost to a mirror finish.

And the expected bullfighter painting over the fireplace.

Potemkin village.

Melendez moved to a sidebar and fixed himself a drink. Sasha settled for some tonic water with a bit of lemon juice and some bitters. He was more interested in the ice that got added, as he felt dry after his already long day.

They moved near to the fireplace, but it was not lit. Merely prepared. Melendez sat in a chair. Sasha sat on a couch.

Time passed.

Sasha heard the man approaching the door, however quietly he might be moving, and rose. Melendez was surprised, and thus still seated when the heavy-set man in the faded green military uniform entered the library.

Tall and proud, but older. Perhaps sixty. Pear-shaped, barely concealed by baggy jodhpurs and an obvious girdle of some sort, desperately overworked. Cavalry boots. Lots of gold braid in a loop around his right shoulder. Medals and ribbons.

Bald with a ring of white hair. Grand, bushy sideburns loosely connected to a brush of a mustache. Sasha wondered why the man had gone to such effort, until he saw the pilot wings over the heart.

He didn't recognize the rest of the uniform, but the one star on each shoulder board was clear enough. He bowed to the man as Melendez finally caught up.

"Major Aleksandr Kryvenko, this is General Don Alejandro Navarro y Garcia," Melendez spoke.

"General, thank you for inviting me to your home," Sasha replied politely.

Not anyone he had been prepared for, but obviously wealthy, powerful, and likely dangerous around here, as *Don* was a Hispanic title of respect that one earned.

"Major, thank you for coming," the General replied.

He moved past them to the big chair by the fire left empty, then waved Melendez off to fix a drink.

"I'm told that you took care of the little problem this morning?" the man began.

"Yes, sir," Sasha replied. "Hopefully to your approval. Melendez has the details and the gun camera film should be available soon."

Navarro y Garcia nodded, then took a highball glass of whiskey from Melendez as that one returned.

"How much has he told you?" the General asked.

"That you had a need of a trained pilot," Sasha replied. "That there might be other work available and necessary later. I'm currently unemployed and scouting South America before returning to Ireland for more recruiting as we build up our company."

He left it at that. Vague and interested.

His audition had been left on the road northeast of Paysandú. Scattered into both ditches, as well.

"These are troubled times, Major," the General said. "Not all affairs can be handled by the government. Nor should they, when it becomes a matter of honor between men."

Sasha nodded and kept his counsel. The New Soviet Man was beyond such primitive things, but much of the money in South America had been in place long before Spain and Portugal were evicted as colonial overlords.

The castes had not moved much in centuries, as far as he'd been able to tell. Wealth married wealth in political affairs intended to keep the underclass permanently in place. He wondered if the General had more than a handful of family members in a house measuring more than a thousand square meters in space.

Several hundred families often made do with far less in Moscow. Thus, the revolution that had ended the Czar's hold.

When was it coming for Argentina and the others?

"How may I assist, General?" Sasha asked delicately.

He was an outsider. And an employee, potentially, though he knew he cut a dashing, romantic figure. Were there eligible daughters he would have to be on his guard against? None could be allowed to penetrate his true mission, regardless of anything else.

"There is another group, Major," the General said. "Mercenaries and pilots like you. Privateers and profiteers, if you will. My nemesis has hired them, and occasionally raids or bombs my facilities when he can get away with it. Today's mission was a payback, of sorts. Something that could be done quietly, and with clean hands, because the aircraft you used is nearly impossible to trace to my organization."

Sasha nodded. The Thunderbolt was extremely common, thousands of them having been manufactured for the war and many Air Corps using them. It would be easy to buy them on a secondary market when they had been marked destroyed in official records. And he had heard rumors that Argentina was in the process of acquiring British Meteor jets to replace their current propeller-driven fleet.

"Tell me, Major, are you familiar with the Werewolf Legion?" General Navarro y Garcia asked.

"No, sir," Sasha replied. "You say they are mercenaries like myself?"

"Indeed, Major," the man nodded. "Pilots, but also soldiers. I am given to understand that a great many of them were Luftwaffe pilots during the war, and that they have now emigrated to South America."

Sasha felt a jolt of electricity run through his body, but tried to keep it out of his eyes.

"I flew against many Nazis at the end," Sasha replied evenly. "They had been reduced to children sent up too early to die and old wolves who were utterly lethal in combat. The Soviet Union wore them down. I presume that these wolves turned themselves into werewolves?"

"I would tend to agree with you, Major, but little is known at present," the old man observed. "How are your skills on the ground?"

It took Sasha a moment to parse that, then he understood with a nod.

"You need a spy to scout their organization?" he asked. "Won't I stand out?"

"Very much so," the General replied. "I have others working to quietly infiltrate. I was hoping that I might hire you to handle more direct options. Break into their facility secretly and find out how much of a threat they are. I pay well, and reward loyalty. And feel like I need my own expert mercenaries to counter what Escarra has done."

"Escarra, sir?"

"*Don* Julio Escarra, Major," the General said. "My nemesis, I suppose, if you wished to be flamboyant about it. Peron rules, but only with the assistance of many and the quiet support of others. Behind the scenes, the backstabbing barely abates for an hour, as folks are routinely denounced, betrayed, and rehabilitated."

Sasha nodded. He'd lived through similar things, but supposed that only the top elements of Argentine society were involved here, rather than even the meanest peasant back home that might be denounced as a kulak and sent to a work camp to die.

Many had.

"They have a facility where I might break in, General?" Sasha asked. "Do I understand you correctly?"

"You do, Major," the man nodded, sipping his whiskey. "They keep things largely hidden from view, both with ground security as well as ready aircraft capable of quickly intercepting anyone attempting to fly perhaps too close. I need a man that can get in quietly, look around with expert, *professional* eyes, and report back. You are a pilot and a veteran of the war, so you have skills and knowledge most lack. And the pay will be very good when you return."

"I will need my comrade Yuri," Sasha decided. "Another expert pilot and old friend going back nearly a decade."

"Bring him," General Navarro y Garcia nodded. "Find me the truth."

"I will do what I can, General," Sasha replied.

Deep in his heart, Sasha already knew.

It had begun.

PART THREE
WEREWOLF

CHAPTER 15

Sasha had considered changing into something green and dark enough to hide, but Yuri had pointed out that they would not be operating entirely in darkness, and that the blues of their uniforms might actually disappear better in dim light.

Thus, they remained dressed as warriors of the Red Branch.

Forward scouts, though they were the entirety of the organization at present. That would have to change if Voss had an entire mercenary company backing him, though Sasha was only hoping and guessing that this Werewolf Legion was one and the same with the Colonel's old nemesis.

Still, it gave him hope that he was on the right track.

It was dark. The sun was just down, sliding the evening from reds to purples as the breeze faded. The moon would rise about an hour before false dawn, so they had perhaps eight hours to work safely.

The General had given them a car that could not be traced back to him supposedly. Yuri had navigated while Sasha had driven, heading further west to a location near to *Santa Rosa de Rio Primero*, just south of the salt lake known as *Mar Chiquita*.

Cattle country for the most part, with old forests slowly being cut down and removed. Not a lot of cover, though the ground itself was generally low rolling hills, coming down from the mountains and highlands as you got further west.

They had driven to a shaded spot largely around the back from an airstrip as the late afternoon sun faded and settled. Below them now was level ground more than two kilometers long and paved as a runway, with a large number of hangars and buildings on the far end away from them.

The General's people had suggested that this was the best location to break into the air base, though both Sasha and Yuri had expressed concern that there might be spies in the General's household willing to pass along a message that there were thieves in the night.

Hopefully, the mercenaries operated to some code, instead of being mere pirates who would execute him if he was caught. Even ex-Nazis, if one ever stopped being such a thing.

Sasha had no intention of finding out.

"Should we take the Thompsons?" Yuri asked.

It was seductive. He'd known the weapon during the war, a safety blanket he had occasionally carried in his aircraft against being forced down in enemy territory.

"No," Sasha decided. "It would be too tempting to try to shoot our way out. Let us be thieves in the night."

Yuri nodded and they made their way over the small hill, moving quickly from bush to bush. The airstrip wasn't fully lit, but there were lights around the perimeter bright enough to see by and he didn't want to stand out if someone looked.

Better they took him and Yuri for coyotes or something, though he'd heard none.

Coyotes knew better than to roam too close to wolves. Or werewolves.

The outer perimeter was marked by four lines of American-style barbed wire, perhaps one hundred and forty centimeters tall. Unwired for electric shocks on closer examination, and Sasha presumed that wild animals nearby would like be a constant source of alarms if they were.

He had his Shanxi on his hip, buttoned in for now, so Sasha checked the ground on the far side, placed a hand on a post, and side-vaulted over quickly.

"You make that look too easy," Yuri chuckled quietly, taking the time to climb up and over while not snagging his pants on the barbs.

Sasha smiled and kept watch.

Long, black runway with **02** visible at this end. The landing lights were off, so he had the choice of circling long ways around or cutting straight through the center. The former would probably be safer, but would take much longer and Sasha wanted to be back out as quickly as possible, so that his car wasn't the only one on the road if an alarm sounded and someone scrambled aircraft.

He'd been on the other side of that equation just a few days ago.

"This way," Sasha muttered, starting directly across, walking down the side of the asphalt like a man on patrol.

If you looked like you belonged, people tended to assume you did. Conversely, if you walked like a thief, people would inquire more sharply, and it would be painfully obvious that he and Yuri were trespassing.

Fortunately, he couldn't see anyone moving around nearby. The various hangars were all dark, mostly with bay doors closed.

There was a large building at the far end, beyond a cluster of smaller buildings he took to be offices and barracks. A factory, perhaps? It had that size and volume, and Sasha had spent a great deal of time inside such buildings consulting.

What were they building? The General would need to know. Sasha would need to know, if these were his Nazi foes.

He kept walking smoothly and evenly, thankful that the setting sun lit his left instead of being behind him where it might make him stand out.

Darkness had fallen entirely by the time they reached the first of six hangars in a row. Sasha inspected the door, but it did not appear to be locked. He considered his Shanxi, but decided to focus on stealth.

Drawing a pistol changed his frame of mind and not in a good way.

He closed his hand on the warm brass and opened it, prepared to confront anyone inside and hopefully bluff them.

Darkness. Not perfect dark, as there were several lights overhead on, but they barely lit things and Sasha could see where several more banks of lights could be turned on if one needed to work at night.

Hopefully, they were alone.

He gestured Yuri in and closed the door.

"You watch here," Sasha ordered, then began circling to his right.

Four aircraft. All old Thunderbolts like he had flown, painted black with a gold wolf's head logo instead of a red star or a swastika. None were armed with bombs at present, but all looked flyable.

A machine shop and crates of parts partially concealed an office. Sasha pulled a small flashlight from his gear and inspected the room. It looked like a place where a senior sergeant worked. Probably the chief of the ground crew.

A file cabinet listed maintenance records for the craft, but Sasha didn't spend much time looking for particular. The General had said that Thunderbolts were common in Latin America, mostly because so many had been manufactured, and they were now all obsolete as everyone was furiously building jets.

Still, it let him see that this organization was professional. Detailed flight and repair logs, written in Spanish and notated variously. These craft, however, hadn't been flown in at least a year.

Long term storage? Overflow? Leftovers when newer and better aircraft became available?

Sasha didn't know. And he would need to. He returned to where Yuri had the door open a crack to watch outside.

"We move on," Sasha told his old friend.

They slipped out and along the front of this hangar to the next. Sasha noted a different smell as he approached. Jet fuel, which had always struck him as having a sweeter flavor over the fuel for the old Lavochkins or Thunderbolts.

He nodded and approached the side door with care. Jet smells suggested newer aircraft and possibly folks working on them.

Glancing at the ground below the door, there was no light spilling out. Hopefully this hangar was as unused as the other.

The handle turned easily in his hand, so Sasha took a deep breath and pushed it inward.

"What the hell is that?" Yuri asked.

CHAPTER 16

Sasha nodded as his eyes took in the gloom. Black aircraft, in a barely lit hangar. Long and low-slung, with wings located amidship and a tall tail. Boxy engine nacelles without propellers.

"In," he said to Yuri, looking back over the taller man's shoulder to confirm that no new lights had appeared.

They had penetrated into a more interesting part of the base now.

"You watch," Sasha reminded, then moved again to circle to his right as he inspected.

The interior layout was the same, so he found the office easily enough. Located the file cabinet he wanted. Pulled out the paperwork.

Much of it was marked Curtiss-Wright Corporation, an American outfit Sasha knew from the P-40 Warhawk and the C-46 Commando transport aircraft he had ferried in from Persia and other places during the war.

Sasha hadn't come as a trained spy, so he cursed himself for lacking any sort of camera that could photograph the documents. Or paper to make notes on.

He settled for finding the title page from one of the repair manuals and tearing it out, folding it up and stashing it in a pocket for now. Hopefully, he would be able to do more research later.

Instead, he moved to the closest aircraft, noting the triangle landing gear and two seats, presumably a pilot and a radar operator or navigator side by side. Beside him, squared off engine nacelles, so he moved closer to inspect them. One on each wing, when frequently you might find two each, but he didn't recognize the exact design, though it appeared to have been derived from the General Electric/Allison J35, an axial-flow compressor design he was familiar with from what Soviet spies had learned and reported back.

Even today, Soviet engineers were busy reverse-engineering various things they had acquired or stolen, including when British Prime Minister Attlee had helpfully sold the Soviet Union a number of Rolls-Royce Nene engines in '46 and '47.

It had only been more recently when the Americans had started leaning on the British to be more fervently anti-Communist. Sasha wondered how things might have fared in the modern era if the world hadn't become divided sharply into two opposed camps, after the Alliance had defeated fascism.

Water under the bridge.

He moved to the nose and counted four barrels. Likely the 20mm Hispano-Suiza HS.404 or a variant. Modern aircraft were armored enough to require larger cannon, though Sasha expected some sort of guided rockets to replace them at some point as the technology improved.

Dangerous aircraft, and everything about it suggested an interceptor, rather than a bomber of any kind, so the Thunderbolts made more sense. Clear the skies with this black beast, then come in low and slow with bombs or rockets.

He returned to Yuri.

"Do we know what it is?" the man asked.

"Derived from an American design," Sasha replied. "We will need someone with better resources to tell us more, but I have information they can use."

"Do we try our luck with the main building at this point?" Yuri asked.

Sasha considered it. Wondered how far they could push.

At the same time, they had surprise on their side. Escarra would know about the attack on his convoy and no doubt be furiously scrambling to discover who had done it.

How soon would he tell his Werewolf Legion? Or engage them to hunt someone down, who might even now be hiding inside their air base?

"Yes," Sasha decided. "Keep watch for a ground vehicle we might steal if someone sounds an alarm, because we would need to flee madly into the night if that happened, and I cannot assume that the locals wouldn't notify the authorities or the mercenaries if something happened."

"Would the General rescue us?" Yuri pressed.

"Nobody is likely in a position to help," Sasha shrugged. "These folks have jet interceptors, and I doubt that the General's forces can resist that, unless they can somehow call in the Argentine Air Corps to intervene. And those folks do not have modern jet aircraft yet, either, so it might be a blood bath in the skies if something happened. No, my friend, we are likely on our own."

Yuri nodded and pulled the door enough to peek out, then slid through, with Sasha close in his wake like a wingman flying tight on a flank.

So many mysteries to solve.

CHAPTER 17

Sasha led. These hangars were closer together, so they could slip from corner to corner quickly. Snatches of music were audible from one of the lit buildings across the flightway, so he presumed a barracks, with pilots being pilots. Drinking, carousing, something.

It helped, if they weren't on any sort of alert status. Merely enjoying themselves.

Sasha could be a mouse in the cupboard.

After the last hangar, there was a wide space to cross. Badly lit because the main lights were off, but still they would be visible to someone watching. He had no way of knowing how many pilots there might be in a mercenary company. How many mechanics. How many support staff.

After the war, the vast armies that had been assembled had been demobilized, leading to labor strife and recessions in many nations, because of the necessity of retooling everything again for peacetime.

At least in the West. The Motherland was still furiously rebuilding from the damage the Nazis had inflicted, and that might require a generation's work. Or longer.

He would presume a normal air corps facility. Perhaps one standing down for R&R instead of on any sort of alert status.

Folks taking a leisurely approach, rather than regular inspections where commissars deducted points for every mistake.

"Come, Yuri," he said. "Walk beside me like we had a late errand to attend."

They set off across the black asphalt, smelling the stench of burned rubber from aircraft that had landed here.

So far, they hadn't seen anyone at anything less than a great distance, but now they would be getting to the places where folks were congregated. The risks would be escalating, because he and Yuri didn't belong here, and that much was immediately obvious to anyone seeing them up close.

And any gunshots would immediately roust everyone else to come running.

Stealth and guile. Nothing else would work.

The building he wanted to inspect was larger than a mere warehouse. More like one of the factory assembly floors he knew from back home.

They approached with care, noting that like the hangars behind them, it was mostly dark inside, which made sense at night.

Hopefully nobody working a second or third shift. And no security guards about.

Sasha decided to approach on the shorter side of the building, ninety degrees away from the barracks with the music playing and dominated by enormous bay doors, some seventy meters wide when rolled sideways. What in Marx's name was someone building that required that width?

Then he remembered what Colonel Nazarenko had said about the flying wing designs Voss had apparently stolen. Blended-wing lifting bodies, much wider than they were long. The Northrop design might require something like that.

Patiently, Sasha forced himself to walk casually. Amble, when the adrenaline wanted him to jog or even run to get a faster view.

They made it to the barn doors and Sasha noted where there was space to slip through without opening things. Gesturing Yuri, he pushed the metal out enough to enter, then slid back along the wall, cognizant of where his pistol was if they were about to be confronted.

He couldn't even risk running madly back to where the Thunderbolts had been stored, uncertain if they had been fueled or winterized for storage.

And the middle of a firefight was not the time to guess.

The interior was a hollow shell, almost as large as the old aerodromes for blimps that he had known in his youth. Overhead lights created individual pools of illumination like holes in the ice that whales might use to navigate the wintry north, with the rest dark.

And the cold Sasha felt was only his imagination.

Two factories were apparent. The closer one was in the process of assembling more of those black interceptors he had seen earlier. Two were currently on a line, one nearly done and one not much more than a frame with one wing attached.

Sasha forced himself to remain perfectly still, in spite of the desire to move. In the distance, he could see a shape, but it was low and wide. A Flying Wing, perhaps? He could only see parts of it over the closer fighters, those long, low tubes with a tall tail assembly.

Were there people in here? Were mechanics working late on some project? Or perhaps merely drinking vodka with their comrades? Any mistake—any attention—would be a critical error at this point. He had vital intelligence that the General needed.

And the Colonel, if this was Voss. And a flying wing being assembled strongly suggested that it was, because the man had gotten plans from the Horten Brothers and the American Northrop Company.

Sasha felt Yuri waiting silently beside him. Sasha focused on listening more than watching. Hearing sounds of mechanics working. Or machines doing more than patiently waiting.

Something.

Nothing.

After five minutes, he relaxed enough.

"Now we approach," Sasha whispered.

"Together?" Yuri seemed concerned.

"If we must run, I do not know which direction will be safest," Sasha replied. "You fly wing for now, but prepared to run if we must."

Yuri nodded. Sasha slipped away from the wall and headed towards the partially assembled fighter first. Yes, more Curtiss-Wright Corporation boxes and crates, some full and others partially dismantled.

Had Voss bought the parts from the Americans? Or had he been so bold as to somehow contract with someone else to copy them from plans?

Sasha couldn't imagine the American government intentionally arming South American mercenaries with cutting edge jet technology. Even Colonel Nazarenko had said that Sasha's Red Branch would appear to be something utterly special, using largely British-derived technological innovations, some legitimately acquired and others stolen, to make him look like some sort of freedom fighter secretly supported by *Some Western Government*.

The engines were marked General Electric J47, but Sasha could see places where they appeared to have been modified, to the point they looked more like the Soviet copies of things he was most familiar with.

Industrial spies, then. And secondary factories working on secret equipment probably.

Again, he damned himself for not having a camera. But he was a mercenary, and not a spy.

At least, not today

Sasha committed it all to memory, and even tore off a bill of lading from a dismantled crate. That went into a pocket and would get him executed as a spy if they were caught.

And he had enough information on these interceptors. It was

that flying wing Sasha wanted—NEEDED—to know more about.

He moved laterally, staying close to a stack of metal shelves holding various things. Tools, parts, ephemera. Finally, he got a view.

Wide and smooth, with enormous tricycle landing gear in place, though the body was currently resting on a hydraulic cradle. Rectangular air intakes, four of them on each side, suggesting the eight jet engines the YB-49 design plans had intended.

Mostly, he was looking at the skeleton of the beast, instead of the skin, but Sasha could see how it would look in the sky, a tremendous oceanic ray gliding quietly along, when the smaller craft brought to mind sharks.

"Hey, who are you?" a voice interrupted.

CHAPTER 18

Sasha turned suddenly to find a man staring blankly at Yuri, having nearly walked into the tall Ukrainian without realizing it.

He had moments to act before the man raised an alarm, so Sasha lunged, driving a vicious right fist into the man's ear and neck as hard as he could. Sasha had been hit there a few times, sparring and fighting as a teen, and remembered how easy it had knocked him out.

The stranger went down like a sack of potatoes. Sasha caught him short of bashing his head on anything that might kill him.

Lean. The stranger felt tall. Blondish hair clipped short. Pale skin.

Not a Hispanic, then. Absolutely European. And he'd spoken in German in his surprise, but that merely confirmed that the Werewolf Legion were generally folks who had left Germany when the Third Reich had been destroyed.

And not all of those emigres were necessarily evil, though he couldn't say where the Legion itself fell on that spectrum. This one was dressed as a mechanic, in a gray jumpsuit covered with oil stains that matched his hands.

"I need something to tie him up," Sasha whispered urgently, glancing around to make sure the man had been alone.

No other voices raised. No alarm sirens suddenly wailing.

Yuri found some wire on a nearby shelf. It would have to do.

Sasha turned the man over and bound his hands behind him. Tight enough to hold, but not to cut off circulation. He took the man's hat, short-brimmed cotton cloth, and stuffed it into his mouth to keep him from raising a cry when he awoke.

The fuse had just been lit and they had to get away.

So much, Sasha wanted to know more about the beautiful aircraft over there, but he had the basics. The scope and scale of the project.

And, he supposed, confirmation that Voss was involved, as his acquisition of the flying wing plans from the American spy had triggered all of this in the first place.

Why did a mercenary company need a heavy bomber? Sasha had the Camel as a form of light cargo transport, jet-powered, available, and easily disguised as something else.

Someday, the Soviet Union would have better than the basic Tupolev TU-4, which was nothing more than an American B-29 heavy bomber reverse-engineered and already terribly outdated in less than ten years.

Jets had changed everything, and the Soviet Union needed them to keep up with an increasingly hostile West.

And to be able to stop Nazi war criminals that were chasing that bleeding edge of technology.

"We flee," Sasha said, rising.

Yuri had drawn his pistol and kept watch the direction the prisoner had come from, but Sasha wanted out as quietly as he could get, so he left his hands free and began back-tracking towards the barn doors, pausing only to circle the partial interceptor to get a better look at the one nearly completed.

Yes, the same model as the ones he had seen out in the hangar, so presumably the Werewolf Legion was in the process of quietly equipping itself with new American jets.

Argentina had begun to acquire secondhand Gloster Meteors, but those were already outdated by newer innovations, though they were far in advance of the old kit from the war.

What would that mean for South America? Or elsewhere, if Voss decided to put his services out to hire? Or worse, was he being quietly funded by the Americans or stealing their technology?

So much Sasha didn't know, and the time had run out to find more.

They got to the bay doors and slipped out, as yet possibly unseen. Outside, the lights had not changed, darkness occasionally split by single lights, instead of the runway activated and presumably lighting the night for kilometers in every direction.

The distance was too great to run for the distant fence, so Sasha grabbed Yuri and they walked towards the nearest of the hangars, like a pair of comrades on some late-night errand. Reaching it, he slipped around the far side, away from the barracks as much as possible. That would be where the alarm would summon hunters, though he didn't know what the response would be,

Dogs? Men on motorcycles?

He had to get to the automobile and get away from the base before anyone launched aircraft, though he supposed that he could drive without headlights in a pinch. It had frequently been necessary during the war, and his skills remained sharp.

Each hangar got them that much closer to their escape. To the freedom of the darkness.

Finally, they faced open ground. Two kilometers with no cover, planed off almost perfectly flat by industrial machines to make a landing strip for jets.

"Now what?" Yuri asked.

"We walk," Sasha said.

"Do we walk apart, or perhaps one in front of the other, to present a smaller target?" Yuri asked. "In fact, I will follow you. If they shoot, perhaps they only see me and you get away."

Sasha wanted to argue with the man, but deep in his heart he knew that his old comrade was correct. If one of them was shot, either they both died, or one got away with the information that the Colonel needed. The General only needed to be informed that Voss and his Werewolf Legion were building combat jets and possibly a heavy bomber of some sort.

For whatever nefarious purposes an escaped war criminal might put it to.

"We will escape, Yuri my old friend," Sasha informed him, then began walking.

Not too briskly. Not sauntering, either. Two men with a purpose and a goal that needed to be completed so they could get back to his drinking, perhaps. An inspection of some sort, clear out at the far end of the runway, one that could not wait until the dawn. Perhaps lights needed to be repaired.

Something other than an alarm that needed to be sounded to deal with intruders who had already penetrated the center of the aircraft factory back there.

He had to get away.

CHAPTER 19

Sasha breathed a sigh of relief when they came over the hill and found the car parked where they had left it. Somewhere, he had feared a truck and armed guards standing watch, pointing rifles at him right now.

"In," he said simply, practically throwing himself at the door to get them away from here.

It was all farm roads around here. And not many of those, because this was more cattle country than properly organized squares of wheat, that good Russian Red that had sustained him for so much of his youth.

Sasha got the engine started as Yuri took the passenger side.

Then a siren cut the night like an Irish *ban sidhe* that had spotted its prey. The night lit up in the distance as someone brought the runway and air strip lights to full brightness.

Looking back, Sasha could even see a trio of spotlights beginning to paint the sky, as if a raid by the America Eighth Air Force or the Night Witches of the famed 46th Guards Night Bomber Aviation Regiment, those brave, dangerous women who flew Polikarpov Po-2 biplanes and frequently turned off their engines to approach German positions in near-silence.

Sasha left the lights off and mashed the clutch to get the sedan into gear. He had to get away from everything as quickly as possible, because this car would have no more chance against an aircraft than those trucks had.

The night was his only chance. Fortunately, they were on the south end of the base and it was only a few miles to the main highway. Sasha threw gravel as he popped the clutch a little too hard and jammed the gas.

The car fishtailed a bit, but gathered itself like a nervous horse, dropping its head and starting to race for the finish. Yuri had his head out the window, watching their tail. Sasha couldn't help the dust he was throwing up, but slowing down was a bad idea.

Either it would act like a smoke screen behind him, or it would draw the eye of a watcher, and distance and speed was his only defense.

He pushed the automobile to its very edges in his escape.

CHAPTER 20

Alois had been having a late glass of wine while reviewing some new contracts when the door burst open.

"Hauptmann, we have an intruder," Wolf-2—pilot Sigmar Schmidt—announced as he entered.

"WHAT?" Alois was on his feet, glass down and paperwork forgotten already. "Where?"

"The main bay near the wing," Sigmar replied. "One of the mechanics left unconscious and tied up."

Alois paused to confirm that he had his Walther P.38 on his hip, then gestured his Second-In-Command to lead.

Things were still quiet as they emerged from the barracks and crossed over to the factory building, where a cluster of men were standing around two squatted on the ground and one sitting, still dazed.

Hans. One of the mechanics assembling the wing that would become Alois's Amerikabomber when it was complete.

"Make room," Sigmar called.

Alois squatted down next to Hans, noting that the man's eyes were still showing signs of concussion.

"What happened?" Alois asked.

"Came 'round a corner," Hans replied blearily. "Man standing there I didn't know. Then someone hit me from behind and I woke up like this. Managed to kick a box and folks found me.”

“How long ago?”

“I have no idea, Commander,” Hans shook his head.

Alois considered his options. A thief? Or a spy? He had many enemies in South America in general, and Argentina in particular. Some of them were even fellow Germans.

Thus, he played a dangerous, double game with everyone, but wasn’t that the entire purpose of the Werewolf Legion? Lead the double life. Man by day. Wolfen killer by moonlight?

He noted that the other man squatting was a medic.

“Get him taken care of,” Alois ordered, standing and turning to Sigmar. “Sound the alert. Lights, sirens, everything. Use this as a training exercise, with the men armed and patrolling in case we flush a rabbit, while you and Wolf-8 launch in your Killerhawks and make sure that this is not the harbinger of a night attack.”

“*Sehr gut*,” Sigmar nodded, turning and starting to jog.

Alois turned to the others.

“Arm yourselves,” he said simply. “We hunt.”

The group shattered like a vase dropped on stone, bodies going every which way.

Alois had eight Wolves with himself. Pilots of the *Killerhawk* aircraft, a variant of the Curtiss-Wright XF-87 Blackhawk that the Americans had decided not to purchase. Two aircraft aloft were four men, leaving him five other Wolves and six radarmen, plus the various ground staff and guards, though he probably needed more guards on the ground if someone had broken in.

Up until now, his reputation and his connections had been sufficient to keep his foes at bay. Who had decided to increase the stakes?

He would have to find his rabbit to know, though Alois would reach out to Don Escarra tomorrow. An attack on the Legion was also an attack on the Don.

Alois practically ran across the quad and back to his office, pulling open the gun cabinet to grab his StG 44, the Sturmgewehr

44 assault rifle that might have turned the tides in the east had it been available sooner.

Chambering a round, he went back outside and met up with Wolf-3 and several others.

"Teams of three," Alois ordered. "Armed. Clear the buildings first in case they went to ground inside, while we push out guards to patrol the outside."

At that moment, lights went on everywhere. Air raid sirens would wake people. Spotlights looking for night bombers.

Alois turned to look, but there was nobody running madly across the field to the outer fence at the end of the runway. Still, nobody could escape that way now, as long as his people were alert.

"Also, one man with each team will carry a Gewehr 43," Alois ordered. "We may need a sniper rifle if they get far enough. Break up and find them."

Alois turned and Hellmuth, his radarman, was already standing in his shadow, along with a tall, bulky sergeant named Jusep. That man had broken his nose and had it badly reset at some point, giving him a perpetual snarl.

Alois nodded them into motion and circled around to the bay doors, noting how someone could enter by sliding along the side without opening them. It looked like someone had, from the way dirt and dust had been wiped away recently enough to leave clean streaks.

"Here," he said, gesturing. "A bottom moving sideways. And shoulders. They entered thus."

Alois followed, slipping in to where the next two Killerhawks were being assembled. Soon, he would have an entire squadron built, and be needing to expand beyond the eight Wolves currently in service.

Many men had fled ahead of the communists. The Americans had taken a few, disappearing them into factories and research labs. Others had taken advantage of the ratlines to get to Spain and South America. Once there, Alois had connections that would draw some in, while others had joined up with folks like Tank in nearby Córdoba, though that one generally kept a low profile, only working with his oldest friends.

Not many excellent pilots had survived the war, victims of the massed armadas of American and Soviet aircraft. Quantity had a quality all of its own when it came to that, even as his foes had finally had enough good pilots.

Good enough to shoot him down over Berlin on that fateful April day, even if it had taken the man half an hour to manage.

The Legion would be Alois's instrument of vengeance.

Patiently, Alois swept the factory, meeting two other teams coming from other directions. Nothing appeared damaged, but he would lose a week or more confirming that these three aircraft hadn't been sabotaged. Hopefully, Wolf-2 was sharp enough to inspect his own craft before launching.

Or he might need to be replaced in the morning.

Except that the roar of jets came up as the sirens wound down, peaking and receding as a pair of Killerhawks raced down the runway and catapulted into the night sky.

What fool had just decided to declare war on the Werewolf Legion?

CHAPTER 21

Sasha had gotten to the main highway and was driving east with the windows down when the roar of jet engines crept up behind him. He focused on the road, ready to jink suddenly and throw himself from the vehicle if someone was about to strafe or bomb them.

Not much he could do except try to survive, but there were other cars on the highway tonight, so hopefully nobody would be able to identify him.

Yuri climbed all the way up to sit on the window sill, his head and body outside as he watched back north over Sasha's left shoulder. Sasha drove.

After a bit, the roar receded, which could mean anything. Yuri leaned down.

"They've turned away north again," he called over the sound of the wind. "Possibly combat air patrol circling, as they didn't even point at us once."

"Stay with them," Sasha yelled back, pushing the speed up a bit more and willing to be pulled over and given a speeding ticket tonight.

He could always pretend to be ignorant of any but the most basic Spanish, in spite of all the languages he spoke.

Anything to get away.
The night reached out and embraced him.

CHAPTER 22

Alois had gathered his troops in his command room. Overhead, Wolf-2 and Wolf-8 kept watch, but reported nothing moving out of the ordinary.

He turned to Wolf-3. Ekkehardt Fischer. Slender and fast where Wolf-2 was a giant of a man, just barely small enough to fly the Killerhawk and other aircraft. The weasel and the bear, as Ekkehardt was just barely tall enough to handle the foot controls on many aircraft.

"Nothing?" Alois asked.

"We swept every building twice," Ekkehardt shook his head. "And had snipers on the roof of the factory and the barracks, in case we got lucky and found a runner. Whoever it was got away before we found Hans."

Alois grimaced.

It was one thing to summon a new foe. It was entirely another for that foe to win the first round, because Alois had no idea who it might have been. Or what he'd been up to.

Espionage? Sabotage? Assassination?

It didn't take much to damage a jet aircraft such that it might crash on its first flight, even when mechanics had inspected everything.

Did he dare throw out two new Killerhawks to be safe?

No, he would simply take all the mechanics off everything else. Ground the Legion for several days while every aircraft was closely inspected for damage.

Alois turned to his Wolves.

"Keep patrols out," he ordered. "We've grown lazy and slack here, that someone could sneak in. Tomorrow, I will have the Don send out a company of his troops to act as ground watch. They will build themselves a barracks first thing, then we will have to act more like a military unit again, eh?"

Ekkehardt smiled with his eyes only. That one was a killer, like the other Wolves, but even then more dangerous, having been bullied in his youth until he could exact retribution.

"Do we know who we are bombing next?" he asked.

"No," Alois shook his head. "We will need to gather intelligence on the ground first, so make sure you have comfortable boots for marching. A new foe has emerged from the fog of war. Dismissed."

Alois was quickly alone save for a few techs monitoring radios and a simple radar system that was more a security blanket than anything. He moved to them.

"Have the Wolves return to base," Alois ordered. "And send a message to Don Escarra's people that I would like a meeting in the morning. They can come here if they wish, but I am happy to attend him at his palace to make it easier for the man."

"Understood, Commander."

Alois nodded. Checking his watch, he could sleep for a few hours, then be prepared to depart at dawn if Escarra moved quickly. More likely, they would travel to that palace in the afternoon, giving Sigmar and Ekkehardt time to prepare.

The Werewolf Legion had a new foe.

Would he prove worthy?

CHAPTER 23

Sasha stood in the General's library as the man entered. Melendez wasn't around, and he'd left Yuri at the air strip with the Camel, so it was just the two of them, though the General had staff around.

Still, the illusion of privacy.

"A little bird whispered in my ear that there were troubles last night," the General smiled with a wry twinkle in his eyes as he sat.

"Someone broke into a mercenary air base," Sasha nodded sagely. "Discovered a few things before he encountered a mechanic and had to flee. Nobody was hurt beyond being knocked out."

"What did you find?" Navarro y Garcia turned deadly serious.

"They have at least a small force of old Thunderbolt bombers," Sasha said. "In addition, they are assembling much newer jet aircraft of an American design. A Curtiss-Wright model, but not one I know without reaching out to some of my contacts. That, and a larger aircraft that looked to me like a flying wing design."

"A what?" the General asked.

"Flying wing," Sasha repeated, watching the man and noting his confusion. "Several engineers have experimented with them, both American and German. All of the craft is a thick wing, with engines and cockpit inside that. It supposedly produces a much more efficient aircraft, better lift with less drag, but controlling it can be tricky."

"How large?" the man pressed.

"Enormous," Sasha confided. "Perhaps fifty-five meters, wingtip to wingtip. And shaped more as a long-range bomber than a cargo carrier, though it could be adapted as such."

"Bomber," the General repeated.

Sasha nodded.

"And these new jets, how would they stack up against the Air Force's new Gloster Meteors?"

"The Meteor was the first true jet fighter," Sasha replied, digging into things he'd picked up or been told by Colonel Nazarenko along the way. "Operational perhaps as early as the summer of 1944, though it was only used defensively then, lest the Germans shoot one down and learn how to build them. The technology has advanced significantly since them, and continues to do so. Whatever the Werewolf Legion is building now, I would assume it to be at worst an even match for a Meteor, and presumably far superior in aerial combat. Plus, the Legion pilots are likely all Luftwaffe veterans with extensive combat experience."

"How big is his air force?" General Navarro y Garcia asked.

"I counted six completed jets, General," Sasha said. "Plus two more under construction and eight Thunderbolt aircraft similar to the one I flew for you."

"And a bomber," the man nodded slowly.

"Yes, sir."

"And, damnably, it is probably all legal on his part," the General growled. "Hired security forces, the same as mine, intended to protect both his factories and warehouses, as well as cargo in transit, though they've grown a bit slack about that. Or had."

"Had," Sasha nodded. "They scrambled jets as I fled. One would presume a higher alert level going forward."

"And you flew to Argentina in a single medium cargo transport," the General replied. "Can you even match them in the air?"

"I have access to resources in Ireland, General," Sasha lied smoothly. "Once we know what we face, I can seek to counter it. Do we know how big the Legion is?"

"No, but I will put out the word to my spies to inquire," the man said. "It cannot be that large, as Escarra isn't one to waste money. Even on foreign mercenaries."

"Is he a threat to Peron?" Sasha asked.

Everything he'd seen about Argentine politics suggested that Peron might make a useful ally to the Soviet Union. As President, he had introduced all manner of social and political advancements intended to uplift the lower classes.

Possibly by threatening the landed elite. How soon would they push back? How soon would the Americans decide that their vaunted Monroe Doctrine required that they become involved?

And what would adding mercenaries do to what might already be a volatile mix?

Or rather, how big would the explosion be when some seemingly insignificant spark set it off?

"I do not believe Escarra is a threat to the government," the General mused. "But anything is possible. More likely, he would convince his allies in the government to turn a blind eye to small commercial wars, as long as nobody bothered the lardasses in Buenos Aires."

The man paused, studying Sasha closely.

"What would it take to turn you and your sidekick into a force capable of thwarting Escarra?" he asked bluntly. "Possibly destroying him, before he can use his new bomber wing aircraft to attack me or one of my allies?"

"Time and money, General," Sasha replied.

"You are Russian, Major Kryvenko," he began.

"Ukrainian, sir," Sasha cut him off. "Once loyal to the Party and the Motherland, but now entirely in exile and forced to become someone new. No longer even a Soviet citizen."

The General nodded, conceding the point.

"The Legion appears to be composed of Germans," the General continued. "One might presume your enemies during the Second World War. Possibly Nazis, as Peron has made it an official policy to welcome such folks, though nobody truly understands the man's thinking."

Sasha watched and waited.

"If they are Nazis, would you be willing to fight them again, Kryvenko?"

"I am a simple mercenary, sir," Sasha lied. "If the coin is good, I will fight."

The General waited.

"But I will admit," Sasha replied, "that there is something to your logic. The Nazi Party once intended to conquer the entire world. The Soviet Union would have remained neutral, had we not been attacked, same as the Americans. When both of us were drawn in, we became allies in thwarting evil. One could make a case that these men might be attempting to continue living their evil lives in hiding. Perhaps building up to threaten Argentina. Who knows where they might go from there?"

"I am a patriot, Kryvenko," the General stated bluntly. "Escarra having his own private army is a threat to what I think Argentina could turn into, if Peron is careful enough to keep everyone happy. We could become another United States of America, done correctly. I would like to hire you to make sure that Escarra and his Werewolf Legion do not threaten that. It might be that you are not patriots, but this is a broader mission, Major. This is making the world safe. Perhaps my operations and Escarra's have as many illegalities and such as any corporation striving to make money, but him possessing an unrivaled air force is a danger that must be met. And met now, when Peron's forces might not be up to the task. If you will commit to fighting, I will commit to recruiting a few friends who see things as I do. Mercenaries can be expensive, but there is a far greater cost to allowing

Escarra and his allies to take over Argentina entirely. Possibly all of South America. Or the world. What say you?"

Sasha was aghast. Shocked almost beyond words.

At the same time, he had spoken extensively with the General before, learning as much about the man as he had both missions, so he had a feel for the old General.

The old fighter pilot himself.

And he found himself respecting the man. Old, yes. A Kulak by any definition. Possibly worn and tired, but there was a steel visible in the man's eyes. An immovable steadiness that said he would plant himself in the middle of the road and stop any enemy seeking to overrun him.

Sasha didn't dare tell the man any facet of the truth, but he could be seen as something of a patriot for the forces of liberty and justice, if you wished to frame it that way. So much of the world was still dealing with the poisons of the landed elite who had only been finally broken by the Great War that had swept away the Czar and the Kaiser.

Was the Great Patriotic War the starting point to end colonialism itself? To free Africa and Asia? To perhaps show the peoples of Latin America a way of life that didn't involve the descendants of the old Spanish Gentry continuing to control every aspect of their lives?

Peron promised such things, in his own, mercurial way.

What could Sasha and Yuri do to help?

He found himself holding out a hand that was quickly gripped by the old General, showing a surprising strength for his age.

"I will do what I can, General," Sasha promised, astonished at himself that a New Soviet Man such as himself would be allied with old Latin American aristocratic money.

But evil was evil. And perhaps Argentina could become the nexus point of a new revolution that threw off the shackles of the past.

Assuming the Americans would allow such a thing, which was always questionable.

Still, he had to start somewhere. Had to find allies who would pay him to hunt down all those escaped Nazis that had perpetrated such crimes against all of humanity before the Soviet Army and their allies had stopped them.

"As will I, Major Kryvenko," the General replied. "No, as you said, Major no more, though I believe that your old comrades made a stupid mistake there. What other name will you take?"

Sasha paused, surprised.

"My friends call me Sasha, General," he said simply. "Past that, I am uncertain. Should I use some nickname?"

He was aware that the Americans had frequently given their aircraft nicknames during the war, and used such things when communicating by radio, mostly to confuse any enemies that might be listening.

Early Soviet aircraft had lacked radios, relying on a single flight commander to lead and everyone else to follow. Only later had they been able to speak to one another in the air.

"You will need codes, Sasha," the General nodded sagely. "Something. I seem to remember that they identify themselves as Wolf-1, Wolf-2, etc. What will the Red Branch do, when it is more than just you?"

Sasha could only shake his head.

"I don't know, General," he admitted. "Not today. But I will obviously need something by the time I return with a team."

"Your larger jet could fly across the Atlantic?" the General asked, waiting for Sasha to nod. "I presume smaller jets lack the range. Would you ship them?"

"I will find a way, General," Sasha promised. "It will take time, and I will send updates via telegraph, so we will need to work out some code to use."

"I look forward to your success, Sasha," the man said.

Sasha nodded.

Now he had to find a way to make it happen.

PART FOUR

THE RED BRANCH

CHAPTER 24

Gennadi found it amusing that he had become something of a spy in his old age, after a career in aircraft, then years behind a desk. Ireland was blustery cold this morning, wind and rain coming in from the northwest with a storm front, but he chose to be out in it, dressed in a navy blue greatcoat—a peacoat they called it in the west—where he could see the large aircraft run downwind once before banking over and lining up on the runway.

Nearby, a trio of new operatives watched the aircraft as much as they watched him, still nervous about the entire affair. How many people appreciated being arrested by the GRU and disappeared, with rumors intentionally leaked placing them in Siberian work camps? All part of something greater.

And necessary. He had to remind himself of that frequently.

The Il-28 rolled to a rest and Gennadi began to walk. He'd swapped out his old wooden cane for something more stylish, in his new role as some sort of rich White Russian industrialist helping fund professional mercenaries. The wood was lighter and stronger, with a chromed steel pommel instead of a hook, as well as a matching tip.

Almost English, he'd had someone say.

Gennadi needed it today, with the cold biting his calves and neck. Still, nothing would stop him, and if he'd grown stout with age, that insulated some. Same as his black hair, thinning and graying in some macabre race, was offset with a new beard he had grown in over the winter, no longer immediately on-duty and subject to surprise inspections.

The other three trailed silently. Uncertainly.

As intended.

Gennadi watched the ground crew set up the ladder as the bubble canopy opened the other direction. He recognized Datsyuk emerge, followed closely by Sasha. The two joined him at the bottom of the ramp, even as they began to move away.

"There is news, Gennadi?" Sasha asked, catching himself from saying *Colonel* in public and eyeing the other three, standing nervously off to one side.

They were all civilians now.

"Indeed there is, Sasha," Gennadi smiled, turning to lead the group back to the main building he had ordered everyone out of earlier. "This is is Ivan Zhidkov, formerly a Commissar and pilot. Captain Lyuba Gradskaya, once part of the 46th Guards. And you will recognize Captain Pavel Zaslavsky, your old comrade. There are four fighter aircraft for you, plus crews for the five including the Camel. What can you tell me about Argentina?"

———

The Irish on this base drank a particularly dark coffee greatly at odds with the stuff Gennadi was used to back home. Perhaps they had enough to brew it that long, but he didn't want to think about the relative poverty of the Soviet Union that he saw reflected in the wealth of the Irish.

It was the cost of defeating evil once. And perhaps again in the future.

They sat around the table indoors, drinking that rich coffee and listening as Sasha and Yuri filled in all the details that could not be broadcast. Nor could the two men simply slip into the Soviet embassy in Buenos Aires with updates.

Not as wanted exiles.

"From there, we retraced our route to eastern Canada and across," Sasha concluded. "Yuri tells me that the Camel needs a significant overhaul at this point, but that it is working out even better than anticipated."

"Truly?" Gennadi turned to the big man.

"The experimental wingtip tanks add a great deal of range," Yuri nodded. "While not slowing me down much or affecting flight characteristics. It would be better if we could make the longer flights that the old heavy bombers of the war could, but I understand that jets will need time to get there."

Gennadi nodded. He'd had a crash course on all the things that Stalin's spies in the West had been able to learn or steal, on top of the technology that British Prime Minister Attlee had willingly sold them before the others demanded that an Iron Curtain be draped across the middle of Europe.

"It is good," Gennadi pronounced, looking at the other three.

Each had asked some questions along the way, but largely remained silent, listening and learning. Sasha would command. Being a former major would help, but Gennadi had picked these three from his original list of five hundred potential candidates. As good as they all were, in the end all of them had lacked that certain something that made Sasha Kryvenko the man he was, but Gennadi was confident that they could work together.

The safety of the world demanded it.

Commissar Zhidkov leaned in. If Sasha was the charismatic hero, Ivan was the logical counterpoint, a man of rules and order. Coldly analytical, even, with Siberian cheekbones and crispy short brown hair. Dark eyes sharp with intelligence.

"Do we know what the aircraft were?" he asked.

Sasha turned to look at Gennadi. Gennadi nodded.

"The American government decided not to purchase the Curtiss-Wright XF-87 Blackhawk," he said, "opting instead for the Northrop F-89 Scorpion. I am surprised that Voss was able to acquire parts, but I agree with Sasha that subcontractors with the right plans and machine dies could easily run off extras. Or perhaps had already, and needed to sell them off."

"Is it a better aircraft than our Nightvipers?" Captain Gradskaya asked.

Gennadi turned to study the woman.

The Night Witches had flown flimsy cloth and wood biplanes to strafe and bomb Nazi positions from low altitude, frequently turning off their engines and gliding silently, with the wind over their wings the only sound.

Among the best pilots in the world. And the most fearless.

"No," Gennadi pronounced. "If anything, the Nightviper is another step up. You will be faster and have a greater service ceiling. I cannot speak to the maneuverability comparison. Where you will be threatened is in numbers. I have only been able to recruit and equip for four aircraft. The four of you. More will take time, and we do not have such luxury. Not if Voss and his Legion have begun building a heavy bomber. As Sasha noted, that is a threat to all of South America."

"And more, Gennadi," Pavel spoke up, drawing all eyes towards him. The man blushed for a moment. "The flying wing design is generally thought to be slower, but also to have tremendous range. If they are Nazis in hiding, could they be planning to attack the Motherland?"

"No, that range is impossible," Zhidkov interjected. "But from Buenos Aires to, say, New York City...I think that might be right around eight thousand kilometers if I recall correctly. Within the outer reaches of a round trip from that base Kryvenko visited."

"The Nazi *Amerikabomber Project*?" Gennadi asked.

Pavel shrugged, as did the others.

"It is a possibility," Sasha spoke up. "Hitler, according to the sources we recovered, demanded that New York City be bombed, more as a political statement than anything. Even more important than Washington, because of the pure symbolism involved. And yes, that is an option we need to pursue. Perhaps finding a way to destroy the wing on the ground. Or in the air if we are too late to stop it."

Gennadi considered his options. He could send the team immediately without their Nightvipers, having them there in a matter of days, or he could hold the group here to train, then ship them and their aircraft secretly. As secretly as possible, at least.

So much of what they were doing with the Red Branch relied on people mistaking certain clues for other things and assuming the British or Americans were somehow involved.

He focused on Sasha for now.

"Let us get you ready to take command of the Red Branch," he said simply. "Then get you back to Argentina to save them and the rest of the world."

Because it might come to that.

CHAPTER 25

Sasha marveled at the aircraft. Outwardly, it looked remarkably like the British de Havilland *Vampire*. Low to the ground, with a short, egg-shaped fuselage and a twin-boom tail that was up and out of the way of the jet thrust emerging.

Walking up to the aircraft, it was a night-fighter design, with a side-by-side cockpit, pilot next to radar operator.

"Colonel, I don't remember wingtip fuel tanks on the Vampire," Yuri spoke up.

"You are correct, Yuri," the Colonel replied. "de Havilland is working on an upgraded design, an advanced model they have taken to calling *Venom* internally, combining the DH.113 night-fighter design with other things to eventually create their FB8, the fighter-bomber Mark 8. If they had more money, they might have already built them, but Great Britain is also still rebuilding from the War. And facing the loss of their Empire. Still, this one will have better engines, thinner wings, the tanks on the tips, and so forth. Test pilots I have interviewed tell me that it is as good a dogfighter as most comparable aircraft you will face. And this model has other, Soviet modifications, including a special engine derived and upgraded from the British Nene, a Klimov VK-1 centrifugal-flow turbojet that is being deployed into the new Mikoyan-Gurevich 15 you have flown, Sasha. You might be able to exceed eleven hundred kilometers per hour, though the wings will slow you."

Sasha gulped in his surprise. He'd flown some experimental craft, including the newer MiG and its predecessors, but this promised something entirely else.

He walked around the nose and squatted down. Three barrels visible.

"Colonel?" he asked, tapping them.

"The 23 mm NR-23 cannon," Gennadi replied. "They originally intended the Hispano-Suiza HS.404, but decided to go with this instead, mostly because getting spare parts was more difficult."

"Not as effective as the 404," Sasha replied, standing.

"Noted," Gennadi seemed a bit stiff.

Probably lost an argument with someone about using western hardware that might be better. Sasha let it go silently.

Instead, he walked the rest of the way around, noting that RB-1 painted on the booms suggested that this would be his aircraft.

"How soon can we take it up?" he asked, turning to draw in the man who had been walking silently in his wake.

Ilya Markov, whose brother Oleg would be Yuri's radio operator and tail-gunner on the Camel when they went operational. According to things the Colonel had mentioned, Ilya was a mechanic, as well as a radar operator and navigator. And trained in demolitions and even underwater work.

All of the team had been selected for secondary skills that could improve the unit. Experiences from the war and other things. Gradskaya's radar operator, a former Night Witch named Yanina Chumak, had been trained after the war as a nurse and would be team medic.

It honestly felt like the beginning of something much bigger.

But Ilya first. Sasha would need to understand the man who would sit next to him in combat. Calm. Quiet, as one would like in someone who played with high explosives. Perhaps a solid counterpart, because Sasha knew himself to be the kind that occasionally leapt first.

"Are they all ready to fly?" he challenged the man.

"Yes," Ilya replied, stopping himself short of saying sir, betraying his own military background.

All of them were military, even the commissar, but they were civilians now. Mercenaries.

A new world and they would have to sort out how to live double lives in it.

Rather like werewolves, when Sasha thought about it.

"Let us take them up and see," Sasha decided, throwing caution to the wind.

As usual.

Ilya nodded. The Colonel started to speak, then caught himself. Commissar Zhidkov scowled. Captain Gradskaya grinned with mad excitement.

"Yuri, you handle flight command from the tower," Sasha decided. "That will mimic operations in the field, when we are escorting you."

He was already dressed for it, after all. They all were, so Sasha decided that Colonel Nazarenko had been prepared. Perhaps expecting it.

Time to fly.

CHAPTER 26

Lyuba smiled as they taxied into position. She flew Red-3, but had allowed Kryvenko's old friend Pavel Zaslavsky to take the right-hand position in the diamond today, leaving her at the rear as Kryvenko began to run down the long runway. Zhidkov and Zaslavsky moved on the same beat, accelerating in tandem.

Lyuba was right on their asses, then backed off some. Beside her, Yanina glanced over, implying an unseen eyeroll, then went to work on her radar systems.

They had both flown treetop raids in the war, though Lyuba's old navigator, Raisa Antonenko, had demobilized after the fighting and disappeared into civilian life. Probably had a husband and a litter of children by now.

Yuck.

Lyuba wanted to fly.

The craft was based on the de Havilland *Vampire* already in service, and plans for an advanced model called a *Venom*. Powerful. Fast. Maneuverable. This version was called the Nightviper.

She had her concerns about four on eight odds in the sky, but Colonel Nazarenko had been convinced that they would be operating on the ground as much as in the skies, and she had been trained to survive being shot down and hunted by angry Nazis.

They grabbed sky. Red-3 had great power in climbing.

Quickly, Kryvenko got them to altitude, climbing at 50 m/s until they were above 10,000 meters.

Looking around, Lyuba felt like she could see all of Ireland from up here. They held level for about a minute, probably Kryvenko familiarizing himself with controls she'd already spent two weeks handling.

Red-3 could move when she demanded it.

"Red-1 to Red Team, stand by," Kryvenko said.

This was why she'd chosen to fly aft. The others had to guess what the man intended. Zaslavsky had flown with him before, so would have some ideas. The Commissar would react logically and precisely.

Lyuba wanted that extra half-second to understand what Red-1 *intended*. He had a reputation as a crazy good test pilot, after all. That had been the final, deciding note for her, when approached about defecting to the West.

Even if it was all a sham on paper.

Someone was paying her to fly a dangerous interceptor in combat.

Red-1 rolled up and to the right before nosing over and starting a dive. The other two were a moment late, but Lyuba was trailing them.

Over and down. Run hard and fast, but level off before getting anywhere near the sound barrier. It had supposedly been conquered by the American Yeager, but this aircraft would likely come apart on her if she tried.

Not that she hadn't done the math and engineering work to be certain.

Down into the thicker air, Red-1 leveled off again, then led them into a series of barrel rolls, turns, and slips, though not with the tight precision of an aerial performance team.

That would come much later. Or never. How often did you need something like that in combat?

She'd flown low and often so slow that German aircraft had to risk a stall and a crash to even engage her during the war.

Now, she could keep up. And outfly most of them, but Red-1 ran them through a whole series of maneuvers, pushing them seemingly as much as he was pushing himself and his aircraft.

Finally, they leveled off. Automatically, Lyuba checked her gauges. Another fifteen minutes or so of fuel before they reached fumes.

"Red Team, this is Red-1," Kryvenko announced. "Returning to base. Excellent flying today."

Lyuba nodded.

It had been.

Now, he needed to find her some war criminals to hunt.

CHAPTER 27

Sasha turned to Ilya as he shut the engines down.

"I'm told you handle demolitions?" he asked.

Ilya nodded as he shut down his various machines.

"Arkadi, flying with Red-2, is a sniper with twenty-seven confirmed kills during the war," Ilya replied. "Yanina in Red-3 is a nurse. Nikon in Red-4 lived in the far east and trained in many oriental close combat forms with various Chinese Communist cadre. Dmitri is a mechanical genius. He is the Camel's navigator. Tailgunner Oleg is an actor with a thousand faces and voices. Colonel Nazarenko put me here because you would need a company sergeant close at hand, minding the store when the five officers were off doing things. Or bringing large portions of the team on various missions."

Sasha was impressed. Gennadi had come through, if everything was that well balanced. The Red Branch might actually turn into a full-functional team, both on the ground as well as in the air, because their flying had been equally sharp and competent.

"Then I will lean on you, Ilya," he said. "I flew with Yuri during the war and Pavel more recently. You and the others are relative strangers, but we are on a difficult mission with little margin for error. And perhaps a need for extravagant violence later."

The man nodded phlegmatically.

Sasha opened the cockpit and they climbed out. The day was cold and already late enough that he could see dinner shortly and a lot of sleep, but he needed time with the Colonel to round out plans and go over some things that he had not brought up in front of the larger group.

He had to be able to trust them, but this was their first day, and it had started up there in the sky, rather than around a table sipping coffee.

The other three officers joined him, even as their navigators immediately went to work with the ground crews on maintenance tasks.

"How did we do, Red-1?" Pavel asked brightly.

"None of you killed me," Sasha teased. "So about what I expect from you."

Pavel laughed. It was an old joke among the test pilots. Not when you would be killed, but how embarrassing it would turn out to be.

Few ever died in their sleep.

"What are our next steps?" Commissar Zhidkov asked.

"Even with drop tanks, I do not believe that we could make the long haul from Galway to Canada," Sasha replied. "The rest would be fairly straightforward, but that limits us at present. I need to speak with the Colonel and see how he intends to get us to Buenos Aires to continue our mission."

The man nodded and fell silent. Captain Gradskaya simply beamed at him, as though irrepressible. She was Ukrainian blonde with Siberian features, a heart-shaped face that was quite pretty. Slender and muscular like a dancer, and a complete opposite of Yanina, who reminded him of a simple peasant, built thick with dark hair.

She smiled and Sasha returned it. Presumably, the Colonel had a good reason for including females in this unit, though Sasha had his doubts. South America was a notably sexist place, deeply at odds with New Soviet thinking that put everyone as equals.

Even the Americans barely gave lip service to gender equality.

On the other hand, both women had flown with the 46th Guards Night Bomber Aviation Regiment, one of the most dangerous jobs in the entire war, so they would likely have better experience in low-level strafing and bombing than anyone else he could have recruited.

And, he had to admit, there would be times when a pretty blonde woman would be able to gain entry into places that no exiled Soviet man could achieve.

Hopefully, she had understood that part of her mission ahead of time and prepared herself for it. Otherwise, there might be issues later.

He would see.

"Now what?" she asked finally in a challenging tone, after they had stared at each other for several seconds of silence.

"Food," he said simply. "We will handle a flight debriefing then, after which I need to speak to the Colonel in great detail about our transportation. And how quickly we can return to South America."

"Should you and Datsyuk travel ahead?" Zhidkov asked.

"While I would like to, there will be much I need to work with the rest of you on," Sasha replied. "If we travel by ship, it might be slow, but it will give us time to learn about one another."

That seemed to draw the Commissar's approval. Sasha had inherited an entire group of strangers. Now he needed to turn them into a team.

Before someone got him killed.

They followed him into the building and the debrief actually went better than most. Sasha understood that the others had been auditioning today, so they had kept things tight and professional. The Commissar would be logical. Pavel was fast. Gradskaya would likely be the crazy one. At least in the air. Possibly other places.

He would deal with that when it came.

Finally, he sent them on their way and located the Colonel in his office, handling some sort of paperwork that was filed when Sasha arrived.

They studied each other for a long moment.

"Will it work?" the Colonel asked abruptly, catching Sasha off-guard.

He paused before answering, in spite of himself.

"I can see the potential," he finally answered. "And the way you balanced the pilots against each other and the air crews to fill in a variety of needs. Much will land on my shoulders, but I believe I have made a few solid connections in Argentina that will open some of the doors we need."

"General Navarro y Garcia?" the Colonel pressed.

"An old-fashioned lord in his manor house," Sasha nodded. "But I got the impression that he is an honorable man. And wore his uniform with his pilot wings that first time, in order to put us on a more level stance than one might expect with employer and worker. At least thwarting Escarra for now will work in our favor. I do not know what happens after that."

"If you have a reputation as a professional mercenary that honors your contracts and is effective, that will provide the basis of your future legend."

"We may have to do things that damage or even undermine the Soviet Union," Sasha reminded him.

"And you will do them well," Gennadi turned deadly serious. "To the limit of your ability. The Soviet Union is far more resilient than even those fool Nazis understood. Like the Americans, slow to anger, but terrible when they arrive there. Nothing you do will change that, unless something so tremendous occurs that you have to break character and reveal yourself, but I cannot begin to imagine what might take that."

"A nuclear threat to Moscow or Leningrad," Sasha nodded.

"Perhaps," Gennadi shrugged. "Your aircraft will just have to hunt such bombers down and stop them."

"What if we are too successful, Colonel?" Sasha asked. "What if the Americans or British wish to hire us? Perhaps to train their pilots or something equally ludicrous?"

"Then you will do it, Sasha," he replied simply. "Whatever the mission calls for, because in the end, you are there to locate those vicious bastards that escaped us with the help of the Romans and the Americans. Their evil cannot be countenanced. Ever. Even Voss would normally be ignored, but he is up to something that moves him from simple emigre punk to a threat to global peace. If all he was doing was building a demonstration model to sell licenses on, that would be acceptable. We might even wish to acquire a copy or a license in that case."

"I will not allow him to bomb New York City," Sasha stated unequivocally.

"And that is why I selected you, Sasha," Gennadi nodded. "You will do what it right, not what is politically preferable."

Sasha paused and considered it.

"I have much to read to catch up," he announced. "How quickly could the aircraft be boxed up for transport and arrive in Buenos Aires?"

"That can happen tomorrow," Gennadi replied. "The freighter is docked not all that far from here, already loaded with a great deal of material, such as ammunition and replacement engines. And things for you to read and burn in transit. How soon will you be ready?"

"Buenos Aires is too far away for me to brief you," Sasha said. "If you remain here, we will be on our own. If you are fine with that, then we can communicate via telegram. I have codes worked out with the General already. I can add more to brief you."

"Sasha, this entire mission presumes that you would need to operate as field commander," Gennadi nodded. "That the best I could do would be to provide remote support here, while protecting you from Soviet assassins that didn't know any better. You will take command and execute it. Now. What are your orders?"

Sasha blinked rapidly, assimilating all that.

No more Major Kryvenko and Colonel Nazarenko.

Red-1.

But he would need more. Something symbolic. Inspirational.

Looking at Gennadi, he saw the man in the same uniform, with the Red Branch patch on his arm. A red stag.

Something in Sasha's studies bubbled up from some dark recess.

The Horned One, prominent in much of north and west Europe. Wotan's Hunt. Or the Wild Hunt/Host, depending on where you asked and how you translated such things.

Was he not hunting Nazis who had escaped justice, in order to drag them down into hell? Would that name come to inspire fear in the right ears?

Sasha nodded. Gennadi watched with narrow eyes.

"Yes?"

"I have an inspiration, Gennadi," Sasha replied. "It is the height of arrogance on my part, but probably necessary for this task. We will all need nicknames of some sort, to further obscure our background, and perhaps inspire storytellers to expand their fanciful lies into something epic."

"What name will you take?" he asked.

"*Cernunnos*," Sasha nodded. "The Horned One, drawing on the stag as our group symbol. It will become my personal symbol as well. The others will identify celtic or norse symbols, as befits our new Irish homeland."

Gennadi nodded, eyes shrouded. Sasha knew that the older man would remain outside that legend. At least for now. Other things might happen later, in which case he might just go ahead and in his mind refer to Gennadi as Nuada Silverhand now, the man who had suffered grievous injuries in battle and retired for a new generation of heroes to rise.

What could be more prophetic?

CHAPTER 28

Vanya had to stop and correct himself mentally on a regular basis, though it was growing less frequent. He was no longer Commissar-Captain Ivan Zhidkov. Just *Vanya*. Still logical and precise, but the Colonel had impressed upon him deeply that the Red Branch did not need a political officer as much as Kryvenko needed someone cool and logical to offset the man's wild charisma.

Many would fall under that spell and be carried away. Vanya, then, had to remind them occasionally not to become entirely ensorcelled by the ruse, lest they forget. Gradskaya was one, though Pavel Zaslavsky was not far behind her, in the opposite direction in that man's case, somewhat moody to her brilliant sunshine.

Today, Vanya was deep in the bowels of the transport vessel, practicing his marksmanship with this new Shanxi Type 17. He'd known the 7.63mm Mauser Broomhandle during the war. It had almost become a symbol of the Soviet political officer to carry such a thing. The .45 caliber variant had almost nothing in common except silhouette and the tendency to fire high from the way you held the grip.

Shorter range, as well, but a tendency to knock a target down instead of punching a tiny hole through them.

The Thompson was even worse to master. And he would. Slowly. Methodically. Precisely. One shot at a time. Then bursts. Then learning how to lean into the weapon and fire twenty rounds with a single pull, the noise tremendous in spite of the covers over his ears and the way the bullet trap had been constructed to stop ricochets.

He was still inside a metal ship, wearing protective gear.

Finally, he nodded and moved to the table nearby to rest the beast. He would need a shower shortly, after the smells of shooting worked their way into his pores.

Sasha Kryvenko stood there with an expectant smile on his face. He'd obviously snuck in while Vanya had been focused on shooting.

Vanya paused, stopping himself from calling the man Major Kryvenko. They'd been at sea for more than a week. Still, it was difficult.

"Sasha," he nodded.

"Vanya," the man replied. "Do you have a few minutes?"

Vanya acquiesced. They were on a ship, sailing south across the Atlantic Ocean. Other than training, he had little to do to fill his days, even as the others were more social.

He'd spent too long as the political officer, watching all those around him hawklike for deviations and regressions.

Undoing that habit was harder than he'd originally thought.

They ended in a small office not far enough from the engine room. Vanya could feel the pulse of the drive shaft reverberate in his sternum.

"I've spoken with the others," Sasha began. "Lyuba is obvious. Pavel is someone I knew previously, as is Yuri. What was it that convinced you to join us, Vanya? Why turn into the thing you hated most in the world?"

Vanya nodded as a placeholder. Yes, he had been expecting this question, since he'd first been approached by Colonel Nazarenko about a deep cover mission that would test him like none other.

But wasn't that it?

"The challenge, Sasha," Vanya replied.

"How so?"

"We will become pickled in the brine of capitalism and western decadence," Vanya offered. "I believe that I can retain my soul in spite of that, but this was the opportunity to test such a thing for myself."

Sasha studied him. Vanya understood that he was the odd character out here. Pilots were generally loud and abrasive. It was in the nature of someone willing to go into the sky alone and challenge the fates.

But even air squadrons had needed commissars, and would not accept him if he couldn't fly with them.

Match them.

Beat them.

And he had.

"You will also have to watch the rest of us descend into that particular hell," Sasha reminded him. "Join us, even. And not challenge me when I lead this unit into those dark places."

Vanya nodded.

That would be the hardest challenge of all. Refraining, in that critical moment. Even if he thought he was correct. Or that Sasha was falling into decadence.

How far into capitalist hell would this mission drag him?

And would he be equal to the task?

"I trust my will, Sasha," Vanya offered. "I will overcome my revulsion at some things. If I cannot, then I will insist that you disown me and cast me out, wherein I will make my way back and resolve the problems in Moscow, or wherever they send me for my penance."

"I will count on you to keep track of the rest of us, Vanya," Sasha nodded. "As my navigator Ilya is turning into my company sergeant, you will be my second in command among the officers."

Vanya unconsciously recoiled at those words, but stopped himself from speaking.

Captain Gradskaya was an excellent pilot, if a bit ambitious.

Or crazier than any he'd ever met. Zaslavsky had that crazy edge as well, but it came of being a test pilot with Sasha before this.

"Why?" Vanya challenged finally.

"Calmness," Sasha nodded. "I understand that I will make emotional decisions from time to time. Intuitive ones, as well, where I cannot necessarily explain how I know that a particular course of action will work out, save that it will. You will challenge me on logical grounds. Force me to pause and make sure, before I leap off any given cliff. Lyuba and Pavel will also need a firmer hand from time to time. If not me, they will need to look to you. I believe you are the best of the three, and later, if and when we recruit more, you will become a wing leader, perhaps a squadron leader, even. I do not know how large the Red Branch will need to become, in order to accomplish our mission. Does that make sense?"

And Vanya understood in that moment why Colonel Nazarenko had selected this man. Until now, some niggling jealousy had beset him, but Vanya finally saw himself in a mirror next to Sasha, and understood where the man had an edge.

Not much. They were both excellent pilots. Both brave and intelligent. Both trained for ground operations as much as flying. Multi-lingual. Educated. Dangerous.

Sasha Kryvenko was possessed of some extra bit of heroic charisma that Vanya could understand, but not emulate.

"You can count on me...Sasha," he replied.

"That is why you are here, Vanya," Sasha replied. "If I couldn't, you wouldn't have made the cut."

Vanya saw the ruthlessness in the man at that moment as well.

That he would ostracize his own Commissar if Vanya's disquiet ever reached the problematic level.

It would be good.

He could rely on this man to lead them into battle.

CHAPTER 29

Sasha understood that he had become commander of a small squadron, but he let military discipline run a little more slack these days, even with a potential commissar watching over his shoulder.

He hadn't been able to articulate it at the time, but he had needed this sailing voyage to bring them all together as a unit.

Zhidkov had taken the longest, but that was the aftereffect of the man needing logic and rationalism to get to where the others had landed after an intuitive leap.

He was in his office, but in the more comfortable chair to the side rather than behind the desk. Reading, but for pleasure rather than more of the voluminous intelligence reports Gennadi had copied for him.

Keeping his English sharp today. Spanish tomorrow. French at some point, in case they needed to be hired into one of the Gallic African or Asian colonies.

A sound made him look up.

Gradskaya.

Sasha had noted previously how their uniforms had been designed for male pilots, but someone had taken the time to tailor hers. Someone who understood dancers, because she was built that way. Long, strong legs with powerful thighs. Muscular bottom that the seat showed off when he walked behind her.

Trim waist emphasized by the belt drawing it all in. Small chest in front, but wide shoulders like a swimmer. Jacket's top two buttons undone off her right shoulder, which was how most of them signaled relaxation.

Muscles everywhere, without any bulk. Possibly as strong as him, though few could challenge Yuri directly.

She studied him equally. Sasha wondered what she saw.

A long moment of silence passed.

She stepped into the room and closed the door behind her, leaning against it, still in silence.

He watched, wondering what was on her mind that she wanted privacy from Ilya or anyone else that might need him this evening.

With the grace of a dancer or predator, she moved to the desk, kipping a hip up onto it and smiling down at him from almost close enough to touch.

Sasha put a marker in his page and rested the book on the shelf behind him.

He smiled, silently inviting her to speak. She smiled back, like this might turn into a contest of wills.

She would lose such a thing.

He waited.

"Are you always on duty?" she asked.

Sasha considered her words.

"Define duty," he challenged her. "I am officially a wanted exile, under a sentence of death if the Soviet Union were to ever chase me down. I am attempting to infiltrate the Argentinian political superstructure, that we might be in a better position to hunt down the escaped Nazi war criminals who are our prey. Between now and our arrival, I have much to do to form us into a unit, though it is going well. Then I will be playing a role with masks hidden behind masks. Duty is not something that ever eludes me."

He sat and watched her absorb his words. Nod to herself, as if measuring the actual against the expected.

"Can you ever set it aside to just be Sasha?" she continued. "To stop being the terrible Horned God for a time, and relax?"

Sasha started to say something tart, but something in her eyes stopped him cold. No, not cold. Warm. Stopped him dead in his tracks, though. Playful, but hidden.

He didn't think he'd seen it in the two weeks he had known the woman, but those weeks had continued to be a whirlwind of things.

"I'm not sure I've had a reason in...many years," he replied after a pause. "Possibly before the war, though I wasn't always off duty even then."

He left it at that, mostly to see where she would take it.

What "off-duty" meant to a woman like her.

"So you might, if you had a reason?" she teased now.

"I might," he agreed, taking whatever bait she was offering.

At least for now.

"And would the door remain closed?" she asked.

It took him a moment to parse that.

Privacy. Things not shared outside his office, either with the other officers or with Gennadi Nazarenko. That was the challenge in her eyes.

"As long as it needed to be, yes," he replied, still watching her.

Lyuba came to some internal consensus, because she nodded. Slipped up off the desk to tower over him some. Not that she was tall. One hundred and seventy centimeters tall. Sixty-eight kilograms.

Dancer's muscles.

He looked up, inviting whatever comment she was intending.

Instead, she bent forward and kissed him. More than hello, but not all that passionate. An invitation, perhaps.

He considered standing, but let her lead. Dancer. Intent on something he hadn't gotten fully hold of yet.

His wingback chair had low arms. Lyuba surprised him by

shifting to straddle them, lowering herself into his lap even as she continued kissing him.

Truly, graceful power.

His arms came up around her back as hers encircled his shoulders, silence and a closed door masking them.

This was not anything he had expected, or even prepared himself for, but Sasha decided that he could be off duty for a time.

For a time.

Even a beautiful dancer couldn't be allowed to turn his head.

Not when he had a mission to complete.

Still, she was insistent. Kissed him with power and passion he found both surprising and perfectly in character for the woman. She flew the same way, perhaps the best of the other three at pure flying, where Pavel tended to push his aircraft and Vanya took the logical approach.

She leaned back and he studied her eyes. Blue, like his. Ukrainian, with Siberian bones, because Imperial Russia had been a battleground in every direction for thousands of years, conquerors coming and staying, before being overrun again later.

He watched her eyes, the gateway to her soul. Saw longing in there. Saw it deliberately crushed under that thing she had called duty.

"If we weren't on a ship..." her voice trailed off.

"We won't always be on a ship," he reminded her. "I won't always be on duty."

Lyuba nodded.

"Nor will I," she nodded. "But I should refrain for now, before I take this too far. At least for a first date."

Like a gymnast, she planted her hands on the arms of the chair and swung herself up and to her feet in a single, graceful motion Sasha didn't think he could repeat without hurting himself.

She leaned down and kissed him once more. Passion and promise.

Then she moved to the door, pausing to take a deep breath

and shudder once, turning from a woman back into a deadly pilot.

They exchanged a nod and a grin, and she opened the door, disappearing from sight and leaving him wondering.

At least she wore no makeup, so he didn't have to worry about more than running his hand back through his hair to flatten it where she had ruffled things.

Reading at this point would be a fruitless waste of time, so he gave her a thirty count and rose.

Perhaps some tea would help bring him back down to earth.

He needed something.

PART FIVE

THE HUNT BEGINS

Alois crushed out a cigarette, trying to hide his disgust at the overall situation. Everything—stopping construction, dismantling sections, checking the parts inventory—had been necessary, but had cost him at least a month of work.

"Nothing?" he demanded.

"Nothing I have been able to find," Herr Doctor Gerstenberger corrected him evenly, his washed-out gray eyes showing his tiredness. "And I have gone back over the entire design in fine enough detail to be sure. And to make a few improvements that will make the aircraft fly better when it is finished."

Alois contained his sigh.

"It was necessary," Heinrich continued. "They might have been able to sabotage some minor element in such a way that it didn't fail until we were in a test flight and it killed us. Remember, this mission will test the aircraft and technology like nothing ever done."

"I understand, Doctor," Alois replied. "And I appreciate that it was necessary. It irks me that they managed to break into this base. That they managed to see everything we had been working on. And that they got away afterwards."

"Do your spies still believe that it was related to Navarro y Garcia?" Heinrich asked.

Alois shrugged. He could do that with this man. The rest of the Legion answered to him personally, but Heinrich was a co-conspirator, more than anything.

The man had studied under the Horten Brothers before and during the war. Had fled to Austria with so many others when those damnable Russians had been closing in, before escaping to Franco's Spain and Peron's Argentina.

The Flying Wing was his baby, a variant of the H.XVIII, mixing in equal parts from both of Northrop's designs, the piston-powered and jet-powered wings. The best of all possible aircraft, able to fly the range he needed and escape again afterwards.

But some thief in the night had touched it.

So they had spent a month making sure everything was exactly as it was supposed to be.

Now, finally, they could start work again.

Alois considered the question Heinrich had presented.

"There were rumors of new people," he said. "That one attack on our trucks south of Salto, across the river, just before that, suggested an expert pilot. Probably a veteran hired as a mercenary, but not retained, since nothing has happened since. Perhaps they were hired for only the two missions. I have asked Don Escarra to see about inserting some spies into that household, but have not heard back yet one way or the other."

Heinrich nodded.

"Should we test our new bomber on that fat, old fool?" he asked, referring to the General who Don Escarra hated so much.

"You get it finished first," Alois countered. "And a test flight at least as far as...say...Puerto Madryn, down the coast. At that point, we will consider who we might have to bomb to prove our point, though I am more likely to stage a ground assault with my wolf-pack. Bombs are a lovely way to keep your hands clean, but they are never as effective as the generals would have you believe."

Heinrich laughed like a rusty engine starting.

"I was in Berlin," the man said simply. "Not at the very end, but close enough. Entire blocks leveled, with people living like rats in the ruins. Yes, Alois, I agree. It would probably be best if a group of communist freedom fighters broke in and killed the man in his sleep. Maybe leaving a red flag or something, just so we can confuse the Americans even more. Let's you and him go fight, eh?"

"Something like that, Heinrich," Alois agreed. "Perhaps communists. Perhaps not. I'm not sure I want the Yankees paying any more attention to Argentina than Peron makes necessary. Build me a bomber."

"It is coming, Commander," Heinrich nodded.

After he left, Alois lit another cigarette and growled at the world in general. It had already cost him at least a month. And this mission was already fraught with peril, where any mistake on his part might cause the Americans to look closer. To see what he was up to.

Up until now, he had firmly believed that the Yankees supported Peron's plan to resettle German immigrants in South America, as a way to tighten control in places where leftists threatened to up-end the entire continent. Look at Central America and all the recent and seemingly-ongoing coup attempts in places like Guatemala, for instance.

Their humor would change markedly when someone bombed New York City. Even if Washington, D.C. was closer and more important, the Führer had wanted New York in flames. The Statue of Liberty a smoking ruin, fallen over into the harbor.

As near as Alois had been able to determine, Hitler hadn't escaped the final conflagration, though that was the sort of secret that loyal Nazis like him would take to their graves.

No, he had to believe the rumors. That Hitler had taken his own life rather than be taken by the Russians.

It was up to men like Alois to see his retribution brought about instead.

And it was coming.

CHAPTER 31

Alois had put word to deed. It was not enough to rely on the efforts of Escarra's people. Not if he wanted to be prepared for whatever asinine stupidities the political turbulence of Argentina was going to throw at him next.

He had not brought the entire wolfpack with him, mostly because he needed some back at the base if something went desperately wrong. Wolf-4 and Wolf-8 would cover that angle. He had Sigmar and Ekkehardt with him. Wolf-2 and Wolf-3 were the best at this, anyway, though he had left his other three wolves in a flatbed truck a little up the highway and back in a stand of trees, where they could respond to the sound of gunfire and ride in to catch someone from a flank if necessary.

A smart pilot always had a wingman.

General Navarro had a palatial estate upcountry. Several hundred square kilometers of grazing land, with only a few fields planted with various grains Alois assumed were for the cattle and horses the old man maintained.

Old money, in a manner of the wealthy Prussians Alois had known as a child, before East Prussia had been ground out of existence by the Russians. They might call it Poland now, but it would always be his Prussian home to Alois. Lithuania had claimed chunks. Those communist scum had taken Königsberg and seemed intent on keeping it forever.

He would deal with them after the Americans.

For now, he had to deal with the Argentine scum.

The outer portions of the estate had been marked by a stone wall that had been easy enough to get over in the darkness. As long as he kept watch for any fields solely occupied by an angry bull, the cows would not be much of a threat.

He was in black, as fit the moonless sky overhead. Wolf-2 and Wolf-2 moved in his wake like the bear and weasel they were.

At one point, they came to a barbed wire fence. Alois quietly lusted after several horses watching him from across the way, but he wasn't ready to steal them. And that was a greater theft than stealing a man's wife in this sort of country.

Maybe he would ask the Don to gift him some horses when they finally were in a position to destroy Navarro entirely. Once they could do so with clean hands, because the man was currently friendly with Peron's government. Friendly enough that assassins would be hunted ruthlessly.

Anything was acceptable, as long as the government wasn't forced to get involved. And they would if he killed a retired general without a good reason.

Alois bottled up his general anger at the world and put it on a shelf until he needed it later. That had been the secret that had kept him alive during the war, when idiotic superiors had made amazingly stupid decisions that had ended up destroying almost all of his friends.

Hitler might take the blame as a fool, but the ones below him had transmitted those orders. Had done the damage.

Had cost him almost everything.

Rather than risk horses, he followed along the edge of the fence until they came to a farm road, the kind originally stomped by horses and only recently widened by wheels. There were no lights outside of the main building, but the dirt was a lighter shade, and the night sounds were little more than a slight breeze and a few other hunters.

He got to the end of the road and squatted down. Wolf-2 and Wolf-3 moved to his flanks, watching him expectantly.

"We must penetrate the main building," he reminded them, pointing to the castle.

Like many old buildings, it had been built in an era of oil lamps, and hadn't been fully modernized to electricity everywhere. Probably the general's quarters and those of his mistress and maybe some of his favored servants.

The rest would make do with lamps. At least it was a warm night, so there would likely be windows open that he could take advantage of.

"Do we kill the old man?" Sigmar asked.

"No," Alois said flatly. "Under no circumstances short of utter catastrophe, because the repercussions will spiral quickly out of control. Others we will deal with as they come. As with the men who broke into our base before, we can leave them tied up, because none will be likely to recognize us later."

They nodded. He had a black knit cap pulled down over his ears to cover up his red hair. They had done the same. Three men in black. It should be enough.

"There," Ekkehardt pointed.

Alois sighted along Wolf-3's arm and saw a likely place, where the main building was attached to another via a covered arcade. It was close to the kitchen, from the maps Escarra had found for them, so presumably a space for servants. Those doors should be quiet, so as to not bother the general.

"You lead," Alois ordered the smaller man, watching Ekke nod and draw a long, slender dagger from his boot.

Alois had his P-38 and his StG-44, the latter slung across his back. The others were similarly equipped. He went ahead and drew the pistol, more for the psychological effect if they did run into someone than to get into a gunfight right now.

It helped calm his rage, focusing on the need to move silent, while ready to kill if he had to.

They crossed a wide quad barely broken by a single light over a door on each side of the patio arcade. Alois gestured Sigmar to watch the servant's quarters while Ekkehardt approached the main building.

Ekkehardt touched the door and nodded as he turned the handle. Alois nodded him in, then slid in behind him as he entered a long hallway with the kitchen down the right side and an equally large dining hall on the left.

Stone floors underfoot, with a rug down the middle to dampen steps. Art on the walls, mostly old oil paintings of men in ugly suits. Oil lamps turned down low, providing just enough light to see.

Ekkehardt glanced back over his shoulder.

"I'll lead," Alois whispered in his ear.

Escarra had given him the rough layout of the building earlier. Nothing written, because the man had been working from memory of parties before the war, when the two hadn't been so strongly enemies.

The General would have two offices. One on the ground floor, where he took meetings and did paperwork related to the estate. The important one upstairs where he would keep the sorts of documents that Alois needed tonight.

He moved towards the center of the building, automatically checking the time on a pendulum clock in the hallway as it clicked back and forth monotonously.

Just shy of 2 AM. Late enough that the estate had gone to bed. Not early enough that the bakers would be up to prepare for breakfast. He should have roughly an hour, assuming no noise or sudden surprises.

Alois found the back stairs where he'd expected them. Servants could move about without bothering important people. He went up, pistol and eyes on the landing above, then turned and watched the second floor.

Most of the staff lived in the other building. This floor was dedicated to entertainment in various guises. Library. Chapel. Music room. Solarium.

The place the General and his family could retreat to with guests and have their privacy.

Alois ignored it and went up another flight. Family quarters for most of the run of this wing, with the General's sons and their families in suites and flats, with the old man himself on the far end.

This was when things got risky, as he had to traverse the entire run of possible encounters without being seen.

"Sigmar, you wait here and enfilade," Alois gestured. "Ekke, with me."

Hopefully, the big man could capture anyone stumbling along. Or knock them out in the manner of Hans the mechanic.

Things had not risen to the level of lethal violence in this competition, though Alois had no doubts that such a thing was coming. Navarro hiring a pilot to bomb Escarra's convoy practically guaranteed that, though wisely nobody had claimed the kill.

Pushing quietly at the margins first. Probing your enemy until you know his weaknesses and tendencies. Then pouncing.

Alois moved into the hallway, staying to the left with Wolf-3 in his wake. Most of the doors were closed as he looked. The hallway had enough light to see by, but not much more, so he would be just another shadow if someone was awake and looked up.

Hopefully.

Someone headed to the toilet in the dead of night, perhaps.

If he was lucky, nobody had such a need.

He still carried his Walther in case.

Now, the danger.

Don Escarra had said that the General's office was on the left from here, two or three doors down from the end where double doors marked the master's suite.

There were also bedrooms intermixed, and he risked opening

a door on someone, then possibly having to shoot his way out of the building, though everyone up here should be unarmed civilians, save for perhaps a pistol kept in a closet or drawer for whatever reason.

Ekkehardt was a black ghost in his wake.

Alois studied the layout. The distance between doors, with wider gaps suggesting living quarters for families.

The first and second door on this side suggested smaller spaces. Perhaps a linen closet and an office?

He moved to the second, bypassing the first and hoping that he wasn't about to surprise the man's primary butler, kept close for emergency needs.

A hand on the handle and it turned smoothly. Alois cracked it inward enough to see darkness and nothing more.

He had no choice.

Alois pushed it more fully open and let his eyes unfocus to take in shapes.

Desk. Chair. Bookcases.

Alois's sigh of relief was as silent as it was heartfelt.

In, and he nodded Ekkehardt.

Wolf-3 paused to scan the hallway before backing into the room. Alois closed the door. Only then did he holster his pistol and pull out a pencil flashlight.

There was a light switch by the door, but he expected that someone would see light under the door itself and come investigate.

That would never do.

Instead, he moved to a file cabinet in one corner. Three drawers. Metal. Locked.

Scheisse.

Would the old man have the key with him? Unlikely. They were at the center of his estate. Of his power.

Alois moved to the desk and opened the narrow drawer across the middle, finding a ring of keys that had him nodding.

Not that Ekkehardt couldn't pick the lock, but that would leave marks. Clues. Hints.

Better to do it smoothly.

It took three tries to find the right key, then he opened the file cabinet and shined his light at labels.

Most seemed mundane. Breeding records for cattle and horses. Staff records.

It was the bottom drawer that caught his eye. Mostly because of the file that was at the front and seemed out of place.

The Red Branch.

He opened it and found his pilot. The man who had attacked the Salto convoy in an unmarked Thunderbolt. And notes on Alois's base, drawn from an interview obviously and written down after the fact.

Aleksandr Kryvenko. Exiled Soviet pilot of Ukrainian origin. Purged by the Communists and under a death sentence at home. Escaped to Ireland and building a mercenary company similar to the Werewolf Legion. Named Red Branch after some Irish mythological cycle reference.

Kryvenko had been inside Alois's base. Had seen the Wing and understood what it was, but there were few details here about what it could do. Or how it might be used. Merely that the Legion was building it, along with modern jets to supersede his older Thunderbolts.

His Killerhawks were so much more than even the Blackhawks they had been.

Not much else, except that it was proof. Confirmation that Navarro had been behind it.

And notes that this Kryvenko had returned to Ireland to recruit more people. Possibly more pilots.

Alois smiled. Escarra had a private air force, so Navarro had decided to reciprocate.

What was it the English poet Wilde had said? *Imitation is the sincerest form of flattery that mediocrity can pay to greatness.*

The Werewolf Legion, and this Red Branch as the pale imitation.

Maybe he'd get a chance to fly against this Kryvenko at some point. The General's notes suggested a ferry pilot during the war, rather than flying escorts, though he had spent his time after the war as a test pilot, so he must be pretty good.

How good?

As with Hans, he had options, so Alois closed the file and returned it, making sure everything looked normal before locking the cabinet and returning the keys.

No evidence that someone had broken in. Had read the General's intelligence files, and knew what to expect later.

Let them think they had a surprise for the Legion.

If he could get out as silently as he had gotten in, they would be none the wiser.

Until it was too late.

CHAPTER 32

Lyuba glanced up at the shadow standing in her doorway. She smiled broadly, then realized that it wasn't Sasha, though they had a very similar silhouette.

Or she was letting her imagination run wild.

They hadn't yet arrived in Buenos Aires, but would be there in two days. Sasha hadn't been off-duty but the once, though she had hopes.

But this wasn't Sasha.

She rose.

"Pavel," she said simply, modulating her smile back to neutral, even as his rose, then fell, like a bad soufflé. "What can I do for you?"

Even her tone sounded harsh, but the man had the unfortunate luck to be standing so close to Sasha in her mind.

Almost as tall. Almost as handsome. Almost as dashing. Many things, almost as good as Sasha, though not the pure intelligence of the man.

Pavel's face landed somewhere with a damp squib.

"I was just about to get some coffee and thought I would see if you were interested," he stammered weakly.

Lyuba considered that she was being harsh, so she relented. Yanina was off doing something, leaving Lyuba largely to her own devices. Vanya was too spit and polish. Sasha perhaps yet unattainable. The rest were largely enlisted men and Lyuba felt the need to enforce that demarcation, lest they think that their masculinity meant they had some power over her.

Too many peasant boys, raised on farms and inheriting the old mindsets.

Only Sasha presented the future, at least in her mind.

"Yes," she said, nodding and taking a step. "Coffee sounds like a pleasant interlude."

She gestured him to back up and lead, as the corridors on the old rusty ship weren't wide enough to walk side by side, for which she was suddenly thankful.

The man might want to take her elbow or something equally tedious.

He wasn't trying to court her, was he?

Lyuba suppressed her shudder and followed him forward, to where a carefully vetted Irish crew kept a small canteen.

Food was on a fixed schedule, because the crew itself was small, almost doubled by the passengers and their aircraft cargo. Coffee was brewed and stored in silver urns, next to hot water for teas. Baked goods could last all day. The rest generally came out of cans or a freezer.

Adequate nourishment, though rather bland and a bit tedious itself.

He got coffee. Lyuba decided to make herself tea. It kept her over here for a bit, steeping, and let her recalibrate her mind to dealing with Pavel Zaslavsky, soon to be known as *Aodh*, for the Celtic prince and figure apparently associated with the underworld.

Sasha had simply smiled at her when Lyuba decided to call herself *Banshee*, using the Anglo-American spelling instead of *ban sidhe*. As a pilot, it did fit, a female spirit from Irish folklore who heralded death.

Finished, she moved to the table and sat. Pavel's eyes gave him away. He'd been staring at her bottom. As had others in the room, though the staff rarely met her eyes when challenged.

She sipped and pretended not to notice how he ogled her. Many men did. And a few women.

Lyuba had high standards. Just like her flying.

Pavel was a pretty good pilot. And might have been interesting enough as a man, if she hadn't had Sasha to compare him to.

"How has your sailing journey gone?" she asked, looking to deflect him from anything personal.

As the only woman officer, she had known that she would be an object of lust, just as the enlisted men followed Yanina around with wagging tongues, in spite of her plain face and blocky build.

Woman. Sexist men who automatically equated that with something lesser.

Yet another reason she found herself lusting after Sasha. All the more so because he kept his reticence, so rare in her experience.

"I have been studying what is known about the Blackhawk aircraft," he nodded, seemingly averted adequately.

"Oh?" she prompted.

"It is a fighter/interceptor," he said, eyes unfocusing as he was suddenly flying in his mind. Rather than staring at her breasts. "Not as fast as the Nightviper. Less range, as well. The only advantage that they seem to have is in their ceiling, where they should be able to reach twelve thousand, five hundred meters to our twelve thousand. Not a lot of difference, but we should be able to run them down if they seek to escape us by climbing away. Reports suggest that the Nightviper might also be more nimble."

"And only a fighter/interceptor?" she pressed.

Lyuba had probably gone deeper into the technical specifications of the aircraft than Pavel, but didn't feel like rubbing his nose in it. Not when he was trying to be friendly.

As long as that was all it was.

"Indeed," he nodded, sipping. "The original Vampire that formed the basic design of the Nightviper could hold rockets or bombs on the wings. Or extra fuel tanks for range. Thus, we qualify as a fighter-bomber of some sort. Sasha took an old American Thunderbolt on that mission. We could do the same with our craft."

Lyuba nodded, smiling blandly. The Nightviper already had wingtip tanks added, but could also add them underslung, though her mathematical analysis suggested that she would want to jettison them if it came to a dogfight.

"I presume that was what qualified me to join this team," she reminded him politely. "After all, I probably have the most experience with such things from the 46th, though Yuri did similar things when he flew the IL-2 *Sturmovik* and later the IL-10 at the end of the war."

Best to remind them that she brought things to the team, before the men got it in their heads that they could treat her like a secretary.

Sasha never did. He saw her as a pilot first, and had to be reminded occasionally that she was a woman. Vanya saw her as a person, and she had no interest in reminding him.

Pavel...

She would have to wean him delicately off the idea that he could seduce her. Not that he couldn't, but he was competing with Sasha in that realm, and came off badly.

Better than many, yes.

Not as good as Sasha.

His face fell again. Perhaps he was seeing the truth of things.

"I have a question on the droptanks," she led him off on a tangent before he got too introspective. "What do you think they would do to the flight envelope, full or empty?"

Again, she'd done the math. Empty, they were only a drag, though difficult to replace, which was why they had brought a number of replacements, and the equipment to build more.

Lyuba settled in and let the man talk about aircraft from the vantage of his experience flying with Sasha. Test pilot work, which was extremely dangerous.

Sasha approached it with technical expertise leavened with impossibly-good flying instincts. Listening, she decided that Pavel's genius was in the intuitive area. Feeling the aircraft move and listening to it at a subconscious level, then being able to translate that back into reports for the designers to fix or at least understand.

He was smart enough, simply not all that educated. And didn't read books in a half-dozen languages to be able to speak wherever he went. His English was passable, but not as good as hers. Same for his Spanish and German.

He was good enough in many ways, but she kept circling back to the fact that Colonel Nazarenko must have included him because he had known Sasha before, while most of the rest of them were strangers.

As long as her hatch locked at night, that would be fine. She wasn't interested in Pavel/*Aodh* as a lover.

How did she let him down gently?

CHAPTER 33

Sasha had left most of the company on the ship for now, including Yuri, while he had traveled ashore to meet with Felix Melendez in what he took to be an attorney's office.

Vanya had accompanied him, because Sasha needed to begin setting expectations and introducing the General's people to folks on his side they could talk to.

They knew Yuri. And Sasha trusted him. They needed to know Vanya, as well.

"Major," Melendez nodded as they got settled around a large wooden table with the door closed.

"Actually, we have decided to embark on using code names in the field," Sasha interrupted before he could get far. "I am no longer a Soviet air officer. Nor is this man. We are exiles, and need to embrace that. Live it. Move beyond who we used to be."

Melendez squinted, then nodded, pausing to prompt.

"My flying nickname hence will be *Cernunnos*," Sasha explained. "The Leader of the Wild Hunt. As we are an Irish company by registration and funding, we have chosen Celtic metaphors. This is *Ecne*, named for a god of knowledge."

And it so fit Vanya, the scholarly type.

"*Cernunnos*," Melendez said carefully. "*Ecne*. Will you add a rank to that, sir?"

"Possibly he will simply be referred to as Commander," Vanya spoke up. "Commander Kryvenko or *Cernunnos.*"

Sasha nodded and watched Melendez process that. The man had the hallmarks of a military education, as well as legal training. Not a commissar, like Vanya, but perhaps a man who had gone to officer school, then law school, before ending up on the General's staff at some point.

Thus, best to get him to thinking about the legal side of things. Vanya's realm, in many ways.

"I am informed that you have containers that need to be moved from your ship to a warehouse?" Melendez asked.

"Actually, they need to be transported to whatever air base we will end up starting at," Vanya spoke up. "The boxes contain our aircraft, somewhat broken down for transportation. We will need to reassemble them in place, so an immediately adjacent runway is preferable."

"Broken down?" Melendez asked.

"Four Nightvipers and one Camel," Sasha smiled. "The larger craft has the range to cross the Atlantic, which we did twice. The fighters do not, so it was easier to ship everything as a unit. Four small aircraft. One large one, boxed up at about twenty meters overall length. Various repair and maintenance supplies. I presume a train might be the best way to handle things, overall?"

"I would tend to agree." Melendez blinked rapidly as he spoke. "What is your current staff?"

"Eleven," Sasha replied. "Two female flight officers that will need special accommodations. Three other male officers besides myself. Five enlisted men. I presume we will be operating on some sort of aerodrome with repair equipment and its own staff that will operate separately from us?"

"That is my understanding...Commander," Melendez replied. "How quickly did you need to move?"

"As quickly as the ship can be unloaded and our equipment transported," Sash said. "Once delivered, we can start reassembling everything, testing it, and be ready to fly, though obviously we will be available for other missions relatively quickly, if the General has things needing people."

He sat back and watched the man.

How badly did the General want to see Don Escarra thwarted? And what shape would it take? Sasha already had the intention of hunting Nazi war criminals, though he wasn't sure if Voss and his Werewolf Legion qualified.

Then he amended himself to say *yet* as Vanya and Melendez began going into details.

In his heart, Sasha doubted that an aircraft like that was being developed to carry fresh fruit and vegetables to North America in a single day, though he would be happy to be proven wrong on that topic.

There were other people about, living in that gray realm where perhaps they merely wanted to start over in a new life, and nothing they had done before had qualified them for Nuremberg or other proceedings.

Thus, the Red Branch was necessary.

CHAPTER 34

Vanya settled his tunic as he and Sasha emerged into sunshine. The summer was waning in the southern hemisphere. Fall would be upon them soon, and he had seen the cold weather gear that came as part of their new blue uniforms.

"He will move quickly," Vanya told his commander. "You were right to bring me, as I spoke his language."

Sasha nodded sagely.

"I have been given access to an incredible team, Vanya," he grinned. "A wise man takes advantage of such things to lean luck in his favor. I could have asked. You knew exactly how to phrase the requests to get him into motion without delay."

Vanya nodded. He was still getting used to a commanding officer who didn't subconsciously resent having a commissar watching over his actions.

It had been necessary during the war, though occasionally Vanya admitted to himself that such things might not have been necessary had Stalin not purged the officer corps and practically invited Hitler to invade, confident that the army the Germans faced was incompetent.

And it had been. Vanya always saw Stalin's response as a stopgap measure. Promote whichever commanders who could fight effectively. Collar them with commissars who kept them from backsliding from socialism.

He looked forward to the day when children were raised to a proper understanding of what socialism could accomplish when the monarchists and fascists were defeated once and for all.

When the sun would set finally on the British Empire, freeing their various servants to live their best lives.

For now, he had to work with the semi-fascists of Argentina, resisting others of the same general ilk.

"Where does that get us now, Sasha?" he asked as they walked back towards the port.

He felt a bit obvious, wearing medium blue uniforms, but it was really no different than being a commissar, at the end of the day. They were surrounded by civilians in various attire that was largely European or perhaps American in style, reminding him that Buenos Aires was a singularly modern city, for all it was South America. A potential competitor to the United States that way, though lacking the breadth and some resources.

And ruled by an old oligarchy that would not necessarily give way easily.

The thing that often made them stand out the most was that their hats were pilotka, rather than the American style fedora or a German homburg.

"For now, we get everything onto the train and transported to a base where it can be assembled," Sasha replied. "I suspect that the General may have small missions for the four of us while Yuri supervises construction, which was why I wanted to both meet with Felix Melendez today, as well as introduce the two of you. I have greater resources than I imagined when I left, six weeks ago, and better than the General probably expects."

Vanya nodded. Sasha had explained it all, more than once, and he could see where the Red Branch could turn into a force for justice, as long as they could hold their noses at being paid by one group of capitalist aristocrats to make small war on others of a similar nature.

Though Vanya wondered if he could weaken the entire edifice if he was lucky, and Peron would be able to make the sorts of advances that would truly see Argentina join the most socially advanced nations, something even the Americans could not say.

Movement caught his eye. Niggled at his brain. Practically demanded that he react, before Vanya even understood what had happened.

Was happening.

In his mind's eye, he saw a group of Nazi aircraft diving out of the sun, though in practice it was a four-door sedan rolling down the nearby boulevard and suddenly swerving towards the cars parked parallel.

Ambush.

Vanya shoved Sasha down and went to the ground with him, even as gunfire began to rake the granite wall above him, glass shattering from some plate window.

Sasha looked at the trouble and nodded to Vanya.

"Run," he ordered, springing to his feet.

Vanya was quick on his heels, hunched double as he flew wing, following Sasha through the crowd of well-dressed people that was only now starting to scream and panic.

More gunfire behind them, but the sound stopped abruptly with the screech of tires.

Vanya slipped wider so he could glance at their rear flank.

The sedan had stopped and two men had emerged. They each wore a buttoned up jacket in a reddish brown Vanya's mind wanted to call gingerbread, after the way his paternal grandmother had made it. They carried machine guns of a type Vanya didn't recognize, all black and metal.

Their intent was obvious.

"Sasha, trouble," he called as they ran.

Sasha glanced back, nodded, and ducked into a nearby alley, not slowing down one bit.

Vanya stayed close on his heels, noting that Sasha had sped up.

"They may try to box us in," the commander called. "We must get away."

"I have your wing," Vanya replied, pushing.

He was a bureaucrat when he wasn't a pilot, but Vanya Zhidkov wasn't about to admit that Sasha was a better man. More trained, perhaps. More athletic.

Vanya applied his will and demanded his body keep up.

They crossed over a block and emerged into more traffic, Sasha turning left, then darting directly into slow-moving traffic with the sounds of horns, tires, and Spanish profanities.

Vanya waved helplessly and kept up, counting in his mind the timing until bullets slammed into his back.

They got across and Sasha immediately entered a turnstyle-type door. Vanya had heard of such things, but rarely seen them, and he felt foolish and trapped until he emerged into the lobby of a...hotel.

Carpet underfoot. Chandeliers. Such extreme decadence that he had to hold down his gorge at the waste. The frivolity.

Vanya chiseled sternness onto his face as Sasha approached a well-dressed man in a dark gray suit, standing behind a lectern of some sort at a wide doorway.

"Lunch, gentlemen?" the stranger inquired.

Vanya blinked.

Hotel restaurant. In a firefight? What was Sasha thinking?

"For four, but our friends were unfortunately delayed a bit," Sasha told the man. "We'll have a drink while we wait."

"Excellent," the man said. "This way."

He grabbed menus and walked. Sasha looked perfectly at ease.

Vanya practiced being a decadent, Western businessman. Or something.

The space was practically empty, but it was that stretch of mid-afternoon after he had been told that folks tended to eat, then take a nap or something, before returning to work late.

"Would a corner table work, gentlemen?" their host asked.

"That one?" Sasha pointed.

The man nodded and led.

A waiter joined them before they even sat down.

"Whiskey, neat, for two," Sasha ordered.

Both strangers nodded and departed as Sasha sat.

Vanya joined him.

"There is a toilet just behind you around the corner," Sasha said quietly. "Go in and sit in a stall with the door closed. I will leave some cash to cover our sudden bill, then join you shortly. We will wait a time, then emerge and slip out the back after our foes have moved on."

"I do not plan on leaving our base unarmed again," Vanya said quietly, rising and following orders, because it was a good plan, however intuitive and unorthodox.

Just like Sasha.

"Nor do I," Sasha nodded. "Go."

Vanya made his way to the toilet. Closed the stall door and stood as if seated. Waited.

A few minutes later, the door opened, then closed.

"Vanya?" Sasha asked quietly.

"Here."

The next stall over made noise. A door closed.

Time passed.

Vanya worked on reducing his heart rate to normal.

"I think we should be safe," Sasha finally announced quietly, as no other sounds had intruded.

Vanya opened his stall and stepped out, joining Sasha in the small men's room.

Fortunately, there was no gentleman on duty in here, though Vanya suspected that might change in the evening, as this hotel seemed fancy.

"Now what?" Vanya asked.

"This way," Sasha nodded.

Out and back down the hall beyond this, there was a double door that looked like it led to the kitchen. Roughly done. Industrial.

Homelike, which niggled at him more.

Still, they went through, into a vast kitchen.

Folks looked up curiously, but Sasha merely nodded and kept walking. Vanya stayed in his wake like a good wingman.

Weirdly, nobody questioned them. Merely watched as they went.

Through and around, he found a storage area, then a loading dock where trucks could back up at level with heavy pallets.

Sasha went down a set of steps, then up the ramp and back to yet another alley, at least two full blocks removed from where they had been ambushed before.

Sasha paused at the corner, sneaking a look before emerging.

"I believe that we should keep to alleys at this point," he announced quietly. "I don't know who that was, and don't wish to encounter them again."

"They knew us," Vanya pointed out. "That suggests that someone told them where to look. Which suggests in turn that the General or this Melendez fellow leaked."

Sasha nodded.

"Safe first," he said. "Then armed. Then we will set out to find out what really happened."

Vanya followed as Sasha began to move.

He couldn't wait to pay someone back.

CHAPTER 35

Alois crushed out yet another cigarette in his desk's tray and scowled.

"Do I have to do everything?" he growled.

Wolf-4 had the intelligence to keep a chagrined silence as he hunched in on himself some.

"At least you didn't get arrested," Alois allowed. "What really happened?"

"One of them saw us coming, though I'm not sure how," Wolf-4 replied. "They were already diving for cover before we opened fire, then ran into the crowd and we had no clean shot. I wasn't about to cut loose with an StG-44 randomly, so we had to pursue with pistols instead. They made it into and through an alley before we caught up with them. The car had circled around, but traffic congestion prevented them from seeing anything. We got back in the car as police whistles summoned help, then circled while watching, but lost them at some point."

"Did they get a good look at you?" Alois demanded. "Did anyone?"

"I don't think they did," Wolf-4 shook his head. "Civilians might have, but nobody got involved, so at best the police will have various eyewitness accounts about us chasing, but we fired from inside the car, so they may not associate us."

"I cannot risk it, so you and Wolf-7 are confined to base until we know that the authorities do not have enough to arrest you," Alois said. "Or to show up here. Dismissed."

The man left and Ekkehardt entered, closing the door behind him before he sat in the chair Wolf-4 had just vacated.

"They got away clean?" Wolf-3 asked quietly.

"Likely," Alois nodded. "My concern is that Kryvenko might have figured out who they were, since he was likely the one here before."

"Are they smart enough to suspect a leak?"

"That's a given," Alois laughed cruelly. "My hope is that they think there is a double agent on the General's staff somewhere, rather than poor physical security that let us read his plans."

"What happens next?" Ekkehardt asked, eyes bright with potential violence.

"I think we keep a lower profile for a time," Alois said. "They will be keyed up for extravagant violence, if they are anything like us, so any attempt we make on them would run into gunfire. Better to lull them back to sleep. Plus, I need to know what they have done, since this man flew away in a medium transport, then returned on a ship. What did he bring with him?"

"We know anybody on the vessel?"

"Irish registry," Alois grumbled. "Hired by Red Branch Command as a transport according to information in the shipping office. Nobody knows anything about it, as this was its first trip south of the equator. And again, trying to slip someone aboard now is likely a suicide mission, even for someone as good as you."

Ekkehardt had surged up, but refrained from speaking and settled again. Alois nodded.

"They will, however, have to unload it," Alois continued. "Take Wolf-6 and Wolf-8 into Buenos Aires in the B-10, once it is refueled. Find a spot with a view of the harbor where you can see what gets offloaded, then report back."

"Are we doing anything?" Ekkehardt asked.

"No," Alois replied. "As with an attack, I expect Navarro's people to be involved. The last thing we need is an air battle over Buenos Aires. I have too many other plans in the works to be sidetracked like that. Watch and learn for now. We will have opportunities later, when they relax."

Ekkehardt nodded and departed as well.

Alois lit another cigarette and wondered if his luck had turned when he wasn't looking. Up until now, he had run free, but things had developed friction and he didn't like it.

And bombing a train, as much fun as that might be, would guarantee that the government would get involved. And not in a friendly way. The military had an uneasy alliance with Peron and his people, but something like that would—as the Americans would say—cause them to circle their wagons.

No, best to do it quietly. Let these people get where they were going, and relax.

Then kill them.

CHAPTER 36

Sasha felt exposed, but it had been necessary to brief the General after the attack, so he had flown to a strip up-country in an old Boeing 247D converted to a civilian airliner, then been picked up and driven to the estate, all the while carrying a small briefcase with his Shanxi in it.

Much faster to travel this way, given the size of the country, but that flight had left him nervous as well, slowly lumbering along in an unarmed, civilian aircraft.

He couldn't wait until Red-1 was ready to fly again.

The butler had escorted Sasha upstairs this time, to a much cozier office than the library downstairs where he had met the man before. The General was behind his desk, gruff and serious, though with a glass of whiskey in front of him and a bottle nearby.

The butler saw him in and left, so Sasha sat. Got a glass delivered.

"I'm sorry about what happened in town," the man said simply. "Your enemies or mine?"

"At this point, I don't know," Sasha replied. "As I become more involved in your operation, the two might join forces as well."

"I have a facility where your aircraft will be delivered," the

General nodded. "And I have added to the security contingent by suggesting to some friends in the military that they might be interested in hiring you at some point. They won't, but it provides a way for you to be adjacent to a military air base, where hopefully fewer people will be shooting at you."

"Hopefully," Sasha agreed, taking a sip of the whiskey. "Once the aircraft are assembled, will we remain there?"

"Heavens, no," the old man laughed. "If your aircraft are based on British Vampires, they are far in advance of anything the Argentine Air Force has available at present. Those fools are currently in the process of taking possession of old Gloster Meteors, based on the British design from the war. My fear there would be someone demanding that yours be nationalized or something. No, you'll get them together, then quickly fly away."

"Are those people allies over the long term?" Sasha asked, only to be interrupted by more laughter.

"Sorry," the General said. "It is rude of me, but you are an outsider. This is Argentina. Your allies at breakfast might try to assassinate you over lunch, then buy you dinner to plot against someone else. Things go well beyond fluid here. That is part of the reason why I felt the need for outsiders. Men—and women, I understand—of honor that I could hire and expect to trust. This will get dark, and I do not believe that I can trust most of my countrymen to stand up for what is right. Especially not with so many recent Germans coming in."

"Germans?" Sasha pressed.

"The Werewolf Legion, among others," the General nodded.

Sasha pretended ignorance and put on an innocent face.

"Peron welcomes them, and I understand the need for skilled people," the General continued. "At the same time, it is known that many avowed Nazis are part of the influx. Again, as a Soviet —or ex-Soviet Ukrainian, Sasha—I believe that you will not be on their side."

"So I am to uphold Argentina?" Sasha asked.

"Not tear it down, at least," General Navarro y Garcia sharpened. "Help me hold it together, because we are facing one of the most dangerous points in our history, as the forces of the past resist giving way to what we might make of this country, if we were allowed."

"What would you make?" Sasha pressed, intrigued.

An old aristocratic general like this man, willing to surrender at least some of his wealth and privilege in order to advance society? Sasha had long believed such a thing impossible, because Marx and Lenin had both preached that such oligarchs would never willingly share power.

And that one French Revolutionary philosopher, Diderot, had once said that mankind would never be free until the last king had been strangled with the entrails of the last priest, making him a pre-Marxist in many ways.

"Peron will build hospitals," the man said. "Schools. Factories that will let people escape peonage on the vast latifundia estates, like mine. He will bring us into the Twentieth Century. I need your help stopping men like Escarra from thwarting him."

Sasha hoped that his shock wasn't entirely obvious. Could he help midwife an advanced, socialistic state, here in South America? Or would the Nazi infiltrators resist, because they saw communism as an evil that must be destroyed, like the Pope and so many of his rabid followers?

And would the United States and Britain allow it?

"And Escarra?" Sasha managed, then took a drink because his mouth had gone dry.

"He is of the old school," the General nodded sourly. "Those people who ruled by divine right in the old days, before the first war. Who believe that their birth and their wealth make them better than everyone else. I acknowledge that I was born to wealth and privilege, Sasha. That I had many doors open to me that are locked to so many others. We can open them all, you and I, if you believe."

Sasha found himself questioning everything.

Everything except the raw honesty he saw in the old man's eyes.

He had been sent west to hunt war criminals. And they were here, but his current mission called for him to establish himself in a place of safety, so that he could better hunt them later.

Had Navarro y Garcia sought him out as an emblem of the New Soviet Man, in spite of everything? Could such a thing take root in the bitter, arid soil of a semi-fascist aristocracy?

Could it bear something other than poisoned fruit?

"I can try, General," he replied simply.

The man nodded. Emptied his whiskey and slammed it down.

"They want a war, Sasha," the General said. "We will give it to them, you and I."

Sasha nodded.

Someone had tried to assassinate him in town.

He owed them.

CHAPTER 37

Sasha found it interesting, being attached to a proper military air base, however differently the Argentinians did such a thing from what he knew back home.

The locals could have used some commissars, though he never even thought that idea too loudly in his own head. Certainly, the mistresses would have been forced to maintain a much lower profile. And the all night drinking sessions would have been far less raucous. Or at least stopped at a more sane hour.

Still, he generally kept his team to their quiet corner of the base, in an old warehouse hangar that looked like it might have once held German airships from the height. Or been prepared to, since he wasn't aware of any that had ever made such a flight.

They had space. And had gotten the four Nightvipers assembled quickly enough, mostly a matter of bolting wings back on and making sure all the wiring and cable connections were adjusted and wings trimmed properly. Not yet flown, but that was coming.

The Camel was almost done. Sasha wanted to have everything ready for a ground taxi test, followed by a short flight test. Then simply taking off and heading up-country to the base where that Thunderbolt had been stored. Not all that far from Voss and his Legion, but not all that close either.

Mid-afternoon. The entire unit was assembled, pilots and radar operators. Plus Yuri's tail-gunner, Oleg, younger brother to Sasha's Ilya.

No, Pavel was missing, though Nikon Ilyin, his Navigator, was present.

Sasha checked his watch. Wound it, just because, but it was keeping accurate time, because the other were present. And grumbling.

Normally, Pavel was more conscientious of everyone.

"Where is he?" Sasha growled at Nikon.

Not that the enlisted man was Pavel's keeper, but he was the man's right hand. They should be communicating. Or Sasha had other issues to deal with.

"I do not know, Commander." Nikon looked abashed, like he was about to draw a punishment detail. "I reminded him of the meeting before he left."

"Left?" Sasha asked sharply. "Where did he go?"

Nobody was supposed to be going anywhere. Certainly not without permission. They might not be a military unit, but everyone here had been trained. And should have known better.

"I saw him headed over to the main barracks this morning," Lyuba offered. "After breakfast. I have not seen him since then."

Sasha let his sourness show. He was about to get angry when the door opened and Pavel rushed in, slipping into a chair next to Nikon.

"Sorry, sir," he said. "I got held up."

Sasha considered ripping a kilo of flesh off his ass right there in front of everyone, but he knew that a good commander paused to make sure he had all the details first.

There would be time later. And he had known Pavel for a few years, so he understood that the man might have gone over to the main part of the base to drink with some new comrades over there. Or do some black market dealing.

They were in a capitalist land, and there were so many things unavailable at home.

Still, poor discipline. And possibly a demerit in Sasha's mind, where he had to wonder if Pavel was already beginning to backslide in ways that might corrupt the man. And risk the overall mission.

Capitalist seduction would get them all killed.

"We will talk later," Sasha growled sourly at the man, watching Pavel flinch under the tone, as well as several others.

Sasha took a moment to pace the length of the front and back, mostly to compose himself.

"We are close," he told them. "I am given to understand from Ilya that the fighters are ready for flight testing, and that the Camel might be there today?"

"I intend to stay up late if it is not," Yuri nodded. "We have a few niggling issues that I attribute to lazy mechanics when they took my Camel apart. Nothing that should prevent us flying tomorrow."

"I am not committing to flight," Sasha shook his head. "A taxi test. Two days before we can expect to fly away, most likely."

He paused and scowled at everyone, possibly crushing their hopes for being ready tomorrow, but he needed these aircraft perfect, right out of the box, because there was always a risk of being jumped by Legion Blackhawks once they got away from the city and were out over ranch and farm country. The Camel had cannons in nose and tail, making them doubly dangerous, but he might still be outnumbered, and had no way to determine how skilled those wolves might be until he tangled with them.

"Will we immediately depart to ferry the craft north?" Vanya asked.

"That is my expectation," Sasha nodded. "We will box things up here and the General's people will see them transported to our new base while guarding things against thieves and saboteurs. The aircraft can all carry a bag of personal gear, plus what we can put aboard the Camel, so plan accordingly. Questions?"

There were none. They'd been meeting daily as things moved,

so he expected no surprises. Especially as they got down to the end.

Sasha looked around the group and nodded.

"Dismissed," he said, waiting. "Pavel."

Pavel hadn't moved, probably expecting to get yelled at. Sasha watched the others depart in quick silence, then gestured the man to follow as he made his way to his office.

"Close the door and sit," Sasha ordered. "What's going on?"

Pavel swallowed.

"Were you drinking or blackmarketeering?" Sasha ground on.

"A little of both," the man admitted. "One of the local pilots was hoping he could take a ride as navigator in a Nightviper before we left, to see how well they flew compared to the Meteors they are getting."

"Offering you bribes and gifts?" Sasha asked sourly.

Sasha knew that this, right here, was why the Colonel had selected him instead of someone like Pavel. Sasha understood why. The ability to resist temptation in the face of Argentinian wealth, when it came to cutting corners and perhaps slacking off.

Much of what he'd seen from the Argentine officers suggested that they saw themselves as a social elite based on class, rather than skill. Born as knights of the air, while Sasha had had to earn his wings and his rank. Had had to compete on a daily basis with a number of other hungry pilots, especially when the war ended and many men and women were demobilized in order to rebuild from all the destruction the Nazis had wrought.

Leningrad might not be returned to what it had been in his lifetime. Not for lack of effort, though.

He studied Pavel's body language. Noted the internal hemming and hawing.

"Mostly American bourbon and access to local women," Pavel finally admitted.

"What have you promised?" Sasha pursued relentlessly.

"Nothing as yet," Pavel countered. "Though I might ask if I

can bring someone for the taxi test, if we are indeed not going anywhere."

Sasha considered it. On the one hand, it was likely safe, as each aircraft would taxi down under power, then simulate a takeoff before shutting down. If that much worked, then they might take a second cycle through the team where everyone took off, circled once, and landed again.

It still had to be right the first time.

And he would prefer Nikon handling systems during the crucial moments, rather than a stranger, though he did understand that Pavel was attempting to make friends and inroads into the local military in ways that might be quietly helpful later.

"It shows poor discipline, Pavel," Sasha reminded him sternly. "We have many enemies here and I do not know who all of them are, yet."

"Which was why I was working on establishing other channels," the man retorted. "We will need such friends, and I expect that a few of these men are destined to high command in another decade."

Sasha could not fault the logic, much as it galled him.

He considered it, then acquiesced.

"Pick a secondary you think will be most likely to help us in the shorter term," he ordered. "A year or two, rather than a decade. I cannot imagine that we will still be doing this a decade from today. Not like this."

Pavel nodded and Sasha watched a sigh escape. Probably expecting to be grounded, but Sasha needed everyone.

He had no margin for error right now.

Not when he was surrounded by enemies.

CHAPTER 38

Yuri had ferried aircraft with Sasha in the early part of the war, before the Germans had been pushed back far enough that others could handle the task. He was used to things not being right and needing to be adjusted in the field.

The Camel was being almost as obstreperous as its namesake.

"Yuri, come look at this," Dmitri called, his head up in the converted bomb bay and a hand waving.

Yuri made his way over, an adjustable wrench in one hand because it was also useful as a hammer and thus he had most of the tools he needed.

Standing up inside, he watched where Dmitri shown his handheld light.

Junior Sergeant Dmitri Yefimov. Distant cousin to the great war hero and acknowledged mechanical genius who didn't want to pilot, but wanted to have his hands in engines and aircraft. Doing things.

"What am I looking at?" Yuri asked.

He might be more educated than Dmitri, and an officer. Did not make him smarter.

"This," Dmitri pointed, then touched. "The cable is abraded, and there is nothing for it to rub against that would do such a thing. Nor is there rust."

"What would cause it?" Yuri asked.

The Camel had flown fine, from Moscow to Buenos Aires, then all the way back to Dublin. Before being dismantled and shipped.

"Nothing I am aware of," Dmitri groused.

Yuri started to say something flip, then caught himself.

Sasha and Commissar Zhidkov had been attacked in town. Ambushed, by someone who knew where to find them.

He leaned close to Dmitri's ear.

"Is it sabotage?" he asked simply.

Dmitri scowled, then ignored him to lean in close enough that Yuri almost expected the man to taste the cable.

The scowl deepened when the man turned back, then ducked under the aircraft without a word.

Yuri fell into his wake as Dmitri walked directly to where Red-1 was parked nearby, quickly removing a few panels and sticking his nose inside there as well.

Yuri waited. Dmitri emerged again and glanced down at his hip.

"Good, you are armed," he said. "Come."

Yuri fell in. He was pretty good at taking orders, and Dmitri didn't seem to be fooling around.

They exited the hangar and headed to the barracks, Yuri nodding to the guardsmen that came with the place as they went by. The two men were armed with rifles, but were more for show than anything. Yuri slept with his pistol close at hand these days, then on his hip otherwise.

Dmitri led him to Sasha's quarters, knocked, then opened the door.

Thankfully, Sasha was alone, though Yuri understood that Lyuba had visited a time or two since they had arrived in Argentina.

None of his business, anyway.

Yuri followed his mechanic in, then watched the man close

the door and come to ramrod-straight attention, drawing a hard breath that looked like it went all the way to his toes and back.

"Commander, we have a problem," Dmitri announced in a voice just barely audible. And not, Yuri supposed, to anyone listening at the door. "Someone is attempting to sabotage our aircraft."

Sasha had been reading. He put the book down and rose.

In all the years Yuri had known the man, he didn't think he had ever seen Sasha this angry.

Not once.

A whole book of questions got reviewed, then discarded unasked before he settled on speaking.

"Which ones?" he asked.

"The Camel and Red-1, immediately," Dmitri replied. "I intend to inspect all of them shortly, then make sure that there are guards posted to keep anyone from repeating their work."

"How?" Sasha asked.

"I found a cable worn and close to breaking," Dmitri explained. "Stárshiy Leytenánt Datsyuk suggested possible sabotage, so I confirmed that someone had sliced it with a knife of some sort. Not a saw, and not deep enough to cut through, but it had been weakened to the point that flight stress would cause it to snap while in the air. Something similar happened to Red-1 **after** I had it assembled, so it was not done in Ireland, nor was it leftover from anything prior."

Yes. White hot rage. Yuri was glad that he was off to one side.

Still, the man turned to look.

Yuri nodded.

Whoever had missed them in town, and seemed intent on killing someone later. Possibly at that moment when enemy aircraft appeared and the Red Branch began maneuvering hard to fight.

"Do we delay our schedule?" Yuri asked.

"How long to fix?" the commander turned back to Dmitri.

"I will not sleep until all five aircraft are inspected and

repaired," he replied. "Yuri can fly with the squadron while I sleep in the aircraft airborne."

Yuri supposed so. And he could always wake the man if they had to fight.

"Do we trust locals as guards?" Yuri asked.

"The only people who should have been anywhere near those aircraft were our people," Dmitri replied stiffly.

"Yes, but the Werewolf Legion felt the same way before we broke into their base," Yuri reminded his navigator. "It can be done."

"Can you have it repaired by dawn?" Sasha asked. "We can take our taxi tests, then quick flight. If those pass, perhaps we simply take off and fly to the new base a day early? It will keep our foes from out-guessing us."

"I will start immediately," Dmitri said, turning and walking away without another glance.

Yuri stayed as Sasha thought.

"That's two," the commander said quietly.

Yuri nodded.

"Many men and possibly a few women might have come through during our work," Yuri offered. "The downside of being close to the other base. And being friendly. Did someone take advantage of Pavel's generosity to slip in and harm us?"

"Anything is possible," Sasha said. "But we must remain vigilant."

CHAPTER 39

Sasha had gotten up this morning and sent a message for Melendez to visit them as soon as possible.

After being briefed, the man had paled.

"Do you think this course of action wise?" was all he'd asked.

"It becomes necessary," Sasha had told him before sending the man on his way.

Messages would be sent. It would be unfortunate, but he needed the General's people up north prepared. And while it might not reduce the number of people under suspicion, it would let Sasha slide away perhaps before his foe could strike again.

He was tired of being on the defensive here.

Lunch had been served early, so that the five aircraft could be given one final inspection by Dmitri, with all five navigators personally responsible for them, and all five aircraft out in the sun where it was much harder to slip up and do anything.

A quick briefing and they would fly.

"Pavel, you will not be able to have someone ride with you after all," Sasha began the meeting.

It was just the five of them, with the door closed.

"Why not?" Pavel asked sourly.

Probably would end up owing someone for the bribes he had received ahead of time.

That was the risk of playing the black market.

"Because we will each perform a taxi test to confirm that everything is working," Sasha told them. "Assuming all aircraft pass, we will take off as a unit and immediately depart this location. The General will have people gather everything up and ship it to us at the new base."

Lyuba was excited. Vanya confused. Yuri phlegmatic.

Pavel groused.

"Perhaps another time we can invite guests to fly with us," Sasha offered. "Operational security today, however, precludes, and I will share more when we land, as I am playing a hunch here."

"How long until we depart?" Pavel asked,

"I appreciate that the original schedule called for us to have lunch, then spend the afternoon testing things," Sasha said. "We are walking out the door right now, boarding our aircraft, and moving. Blame your unyielding, pain-in-the-ass commander when your friends wish to bitch about it later."

He offered a smile, but Pavel was having none of it.

So be it.

"Questions?" He looked around. "Then to your aircraft like this was as emergency drill."

Sasha was already moving, jogging for the door with Yuri close on his wing and the others catching up.

The morning was glorious, with no clouds anywhere and visibility measured in infinities.

Ilya was already aboard when Sasha climbed in and the ground crew began final efforts, the chocks being pulled as Sasha got the engine roaring with a bang.

He buckled himself in, closed them up, and keyed the radio.

"Red Branch, this is *Cernunnos*, aboard Red-1," he announced. "Beginning taxi now."

He brought the throttle up and began to roll. The strip was long and well-maintained. Paved in the last year or so, or at least resurfaced when he had walked it a few days ago to inspect.

Smooth.

Red-1 seemed excited to fly. He got to the end of taxiway and got his clearance from the tower, so Sasha rolled out and lined up, glancing over at where Vanya and Pavel and Lyuba were like ducks behind him, with Yuri last, watching over them as a mother hen.

Throttle up, they began to run. Static tests had been fine. Dmitri had reset and recalibrated everything overnight.

They rolled.

Smooth. Clean.

Sasha wanted to get airborne, but shut down and let the aircraft coast, setting his brakes, then turning at the far end and clearing the way.

One by one, each tested their craft, and everything passed. They taxied down and lined it up again.

"Red Branch, this is Red-1," he announced. "Stand by for flight test."

This time, Sasha let the engines roar. Red-1 leapt into the sky and climbed hard and fast, like a hungry hawk.

Because it had been that kind of day, he reached down and armed the cannons, then turned to Ilya.

"Confirm our perimeter and stand by for hostile aircraft," Sasha said simply.

Ilya nodded and moved to his radar with short, efficient motions.

Red-2 joined them quickly. Then Red-4, since Pavel and Lyuba had seemingly adjusted their flying diamond permanently.

Sasha was fine with that, as long as everyone worked as a team.

Below them, Yuri began to roll. Sasha swept out to the south, bringing the other three with him in a stacked diamond that had *Banshee* up where he could see her over his high tail if he looked.

They swept in overhead as the Camel climbed up, then slipped in just ahead of him as Yuri got to altitude.

"Ilya, what is our perimeter like?" Sasha asked, wondering if they were facing predators above, or if he had stolen a march.

"Individual aircraft," Ilya replied. "Mostly piston-powered, from the slow speeds. I am not seeing anything like a squadron formation anywhere close."

Sasha nodded.

Maybe, just maybe, he had gotten lucky, moving unexpectedly.

Hopefully, it would be enough.

"Red Branch, this is *Cernunnos*," he said on the radio. "Maintain formation and keep watch on your radar. We will be on the ground at our new base in under an hour."

After all, they were cruising at seven hundred and fifty kph right now, faster than anything he had flown during the war could achieve anywhere except a long, hard dive that ripped the wings off.

But they had survived the war and made it into a new future.

The Jet Age.

How many of them would survive it?

PART SIX

THE DANCE

CHAPTER 40

Alois snarled a profanity so loud and vile that even Ekkehardt flinched under the tone.

"How could this happen?" he demanded angrily.

Ekkehardt shrugged.

"Our insider said tomorrow," Wolf-3 finally replied. "Tests today, but nothing significant. Tomorrow, they would pack everything up and move. Except that our man never gave us a heads up today. We relied on other spies, over in the Argentinian barracks, to notify us when all five took off instead of flying individual test runs. By the time word got back to us, they had already landed at their new base. And someone is taking their business seriously because that one has a few old German *Fliegerabwehrkanone* 8.8 cm Flak 37 handy, ready to kill bombers, low-strafing aircraft, or even tanks if we decided to launch a ground assault. Not a lot we can do at this point."

"Are we betrayed?" Alois asked.

That was all that really mattered.

"I don't think so," Wolf-3 replied. "The General's people went from calm to emergency activity mid-morning, so I'm guessing, at least until we find out for sure, that Kryvenko sent them a quiet message, then immediately took off and flew away."

"And none of the aircraft crashed," Alois noted.

Again, the shrug.

"Maybe the damage wasn't enough to happen in normal flight," Wolf-3 offered.

"Or they found it and fixed it," Alois noted. "That would be a good reason to suddenly leave that base and go elsewhere."

"When I can get a message in, I expect to find out more," Ekkehardt replied evenly.

"Do that," Alois ordered. "In fact, make it a point to get him a message and find out what is going on. I don't like surprises and Kryvenko keeps managing to do that."

"Immediately, sir," Ekkehardt replied, then he was gone.

Alois lit a cigarette and had smoked about half of it when Dr. Gerstenberger entered.

"You heard?" the man asked as he sat.

"The Red Branch pulled a fast one on us," Alois nodded.

"Does that change our timing?" Gerstenberger asked.

"How close are you?" Alois asked back.

"Perhaps a week, because you have had no alacrity about moving," the man replied. "We're assembled and fine-tuning things. I could probably run our first test flight tomorrow if you desired. I hadn't planned it, because I expected all of you to be off doing other things tomorrow, when I need a chase plane or two watching external operations."

"And we would have been," Alois growled sulkily. "Two of the five aircraft would have likely suffered critical mechanical failures when we jumped them, leaving the other three at our mercy and the Red Branch destroyed entirely."

He finished the cigarette and crushed it out, resetting his plans.

"Can you be ready for the long test flight tomorrow?" he asked.

"I'll need to do a few things this afternoon and tonight, but nothing major," Gerstenberger nodded. "How loaded should we be?"

"Leave off all the bombs for now," Alois said. "Calculate fuel efficiency when we return, then use that to provide us with as many bombs as we can carry and still return safely. I'd hate to have to ditch the aircraft somewhere on the way home, or land at an unexpected place along the way where someone might decide to steal my Flying Wing."

"Agreed," Gerstenberger nodded.

"And what is the weather forecast, both south as well as north?" Alois pressed.

"Clear weather here," Gerstenberger replied. "End of summer in the south means spring up north. Hurricane season does not begin until later, but we might encounter rain or storm fronts between here and there. I will cable a few, strategic places and estimate what we should expect over the next...week or so?"

"Yes," Alois nodded. "I feel like we will need to move quickly to bomb New York City, then return here and deal with Navarro's mercenaries. I would do it now, but he was obviously expecting something, which was why he moved early."

"Do they know we are behind it?" Gerstenberger asked.

"Doubtful," Alois said. "On the other hand, they do know that someone is hunting them now. And probably that someone touched their aircraft and possibly sabotaged them, if they moved early. We need to move early again, before they can settle and plan their next attack on us."

"It becomes a game of cat and mouse?"

Alois shrugged.

"Possibly more a game of which of us will have a chair when the music stops playing, than anything," he replied. "I intend it to be us, so we must move quickly and decisively."

"The bomber will be ready to test tomorrow, Commander," Gerstenberger nodded, rising. "Then a day or two and we can set out to avenge the Fatherland."

"See to it," Alois ordered.

What was this Soviet punk up to next?

CHAPTER 41

Sasha had kept his force on alert. And notified the General's troops that they should be prepared for someone to come over the wire in a combined forces operation with Thunderbolts dropping bombs and rocketing the place.

A few gulps. A few phlegmatic nods. One man smiled. Probably a gunner on an 88mm air defense cannon looking forward to having fun.

Leaving Vanya in charge, Sasha had been driven to see the General. Escorted upstairs to that other office, so he had moved up to being a trusted lieutenant of the man now.

For what it was worth.

"Sabotage?" the General asked when Sasha was done talking.

"Indeed," Sasha agreed. "I feel like I should do something against the Werewolf Legion, but if they are the ones behind it, they will be prepared for anything I do."

"Yes," the man said. "They may be baiting a trap for you."

A sudden knock and the door opened. A captain Sasha didn't know entered and placed a folded note on the desk, nodded, and withdrew.

Sasha waited as the General read the note, then handed it to Sasha.

Oh, interesting.

"Has the Flying Wing taken off before?" he asked.

"Once, that I am aware of," the General replied. "There might have been night flights, but even then we might have noticed."

"Your spotter said they flew south?" Sasha continued. "Is there anything in that direction, assuming they weren't moving to bomb some enemy of theirs?"

"That is probably me," the old man chuckled. "This feels more like a long-duration test flight, if they took off, lined up a spot, and flew in that direction until they were out of sight."

Sasha paused and reviewed what he could remember of Colonel Nazarenko's briefing notes. The ones he had burned aboard the ship so nobody could accuse him of being a spy later.

He studied General Navarro y Garcia, and saw the man who might have flown duels in the First War, had he been English or German. The sharp eyes. The steady hands. The flight wings that dominated the spot over his heart.

"General, I have a question that might be uncomfortable," Sasha said, waiting for the man to nod.

"I am aware of two Flying Wing designs," Sasha continued. "One based on work by the American Northrop, and the other derived from the German Horten Brothers, one of whom I seem to remember lives somewhere in Argentina, though I am not certain where and haven't bothered to look."

"If you say so, Sasha," the man replied neutrally. Not giving anything away.

"One of the things about a blended wing design like that is supposedly a fantastic fuel efficiency in the air," Sasha said. "Flight controls are supposedly complicated to the point that I know of no Soviet designers who worked seriously with them, beyond the fanciful dreams of men like Cheranovsky."

"Efficiency?" the General asked.

"Extremely long range becomes possible," Sasha nodded. "If that wing was a bomber, there are targets out there that do not know they are at risk."

"Such as?"

"Hitler and Goering both dreamed of bombing New York City, using aircraft based in France," Sasha replied. "I have seen plans that were created, but never built because by the time it became important, the Nazi War Machine had been ground down and they lacked the resources to build such an aircraft."

"It is a little over five thousand miles from Buenos Aires to New York City," General Navarro y Garcia noted. "Perhaps almost exactly five thousand from their base outside Cordoba. Did those aircraft have such range?"

"The Horten Brothers designed their H.XVIII as a submission to the Luftwaffe, General," Sasha explained. "I have seen the frame on the ground. It looks similar to that aircraft."

"What are you suggesting, Sasha?" the man asked.

"Are they intending to bomb someplace like New York City, from deep in Argentina?" Sasha asked. "The flight would take a considerable amount of time to complete, but much of it could be done over water, once they left South America. Similarly, they could escape in darkness out over the water if they were careful and return."

"What do you know that I do not, Sasha?" the old man asked pointedly, eyes cruel and mouth pursed.

"I am—was—a loyal Soviet citizen until everything happened, General," Sasha explained. "I helped stop the Nazis from conquering the world. You have noted that the Werewolf Legion appears to be made up exclusively of German pilots and flight crews. The Red Branch is ex-Soviet, because many of us suddenly got purged, though we escaped with our lives and friends could get us to neutral countries like Ireland. Why build a heavy bomber with extreme range, when it is so much easier to build other craft? More of their Blackhawks or perhaps medium bombers that would be far more useful and effective in mercenary wars. I do not trust these Germans. Especially not after the troubles I have had since I returned."

He watched the old man lean back in his chair and think, a glass of whiskey in on hand occasionally sipped down slowly.

Sasha wanted to tell him more. Tell him about the stolen plans. About some of those men that had escaped as part of the Ratlines. The things that Colonel Nazarenko had known or suspected about how the Werewolf Legion was some sort of Third Reich holdover.

A Fourth Reich, perhaps? Built up in South America and hidden among all the immigrants?

Werewolf. Man by day, ruthless killer by night?

The Colonel had been convinced that the Legion was a Nazi front, possibly still fighting the last war.

And they needed to be stopped, if the world was finally going to be safe, in spite of the rightists who would rather surrender to fascism than admit that socialism was the future.

"Could you break into their base again, Sasha?" the General finally asked.

"I'm not sure what evidence I might find that proves my point, one way or the other, General," Sasha replied. "I fear that it will simply be on the BBC Evening Report that terrorists had attacked New York, though I'm not sure how much much tonnage of ordnance they could carry that distance."

"Anything is bad, Sasha," the man said. "It would either draw the Americans into a war in Argentina to overthrow Peron, or escalate the ongoing complexities with the Soviet Union in Europe. Or Asia, where it looks like the Chinese Communists seem to be successfully routing the Nationalists under Chiang Kai-shek. More wars are coming, Sasha."

"All the more reason to stop them here and now," Sasha said. "Do we launch a surprise attack on their base?"

"Even I cannot justify open warfare," the General shook his head. "If you find something, anything that I can take to the authorities to justify our action, we should be able to shut the Legion down officially. Right now, it is all speculation on our part."

Sasha noted that the old man had joined him in his assumptions, rather than suggesting that Sasha was driving everything himself.

Still, he had to move. And do it in a way that didn't get him arrested by the authorities that already didn't like the Soviet Union. His exile state wouldn't protect him, because nobody would speak on his behalf save the General, who would be equally implicated.

"I will find something, General," Sasha promised. "We will find a way."

He rose and the man joined him, shaking hands across the desk.

If Voss was testing his new bomber, they didn't have long to stop him, whatever the man's plans were.

CHAPTER 42

Sasha had gotten to see the Flying Wing return and land, though he had remained at a safe distance, watching through binoculars that didn't show him anything more than he already knew.

Smooth flight. Eight engines internal, when some of the designs he had seen had included external nacelles that would increase drag, though they would improve internal capacity for bombs.

One heavy bomber was not going to do significant physical damage by itself.

Unless there was some sort of atomic weapon involved. They hadn't stolen something from the Americans, had they? Nobody else, as far as Sasha knew, had atomic weaponry, though there were rumors that Soviet scientists were supposedly close.

All the more reason to stop them. A single load of small bombs would create enough panic. If New York City was about to obliterated, it would plunge the entire world into a war even worse than the one they had only escaped from three years ago.

He simply had to get inside their base somehow. Had to find some sort of clue or intelligence as to what Voss and his Legion had planned.

The very future of humanity might hinge on it.

Worse, he couldn't take the entire team. Every extra person he brought heightened the risk of discovery and capture. One, and only one besides himself? Or did he have to go alone?

These thoughts almost paralyzed him as the driver took them back to Red Branch Base, as it was called informally now. Sasha noted how the guards were all far more alert than they had been when he and Yuri had flown from this place before. They understood that there might be a war coming, from the way they walked with precision and noisy banter was kept under tighter control.

Almost exactly the opposite of what things had been like back at Buenos Aires. Was the military that corrupt and ineffective? Or did the General simply have better troops, in addition to hiring himself a mercenary company?

The car rolled up to the barracks and Sasha emerged, noting again armed soldiers watching all directions.

It was good.

Inside, he found Yuri and Lyuba. Runners went for Vanya and Pavel, until the five of them were gathered.

"It flies well, if somewhat slow, but I take that for testing more than anything," he told them as they gathered. "We must stop it from taking off on whatever mission they have in mind."

Sasha kept his misgivings about atomic weaponry to himself. Surely the Americans kept tight enough security around such things as to not simply lose an atomic bomb, right?

"We could bomb the place," Pavel offered.

"If we didn't mind getting shot down in the process," Yuri replied. "I've seen the 20mm Oerlikon cannons they have protecting them."

Sasha nodded.

"We need to get inside," he said. "Need to see what preparations they have made. That will tell us what they are doing next. And how soon. I cannot take the entire team with me, as it will cause too much noise."

"Oleg is a gifted actor," Yuri noted. "He could fool people."

Sasha shook his head.

"They likely know everyone inside, and would react badly to any strangers, at least long enough to cause trouble," he replied.

"Do you take Ilya as a demolitions expert, or Nikon who has studied Chinese fighting styles?" Vanya asked.

Sasha considered it.

"Ilya," he said. "That way, only one flight crew is broken up if you have to act later. Still, I think that Vanya, you and Arkadi should be close, you acting as his spotter and him with his sniper rifle. I'm not sure what good it would do, but I cannot know what will happen until we are in the thick of it."

"The rest of us?" Yuri asked.

"You stay here, ready act or react, depending," Sasha replied.

"For?" Lyuba asked.

"For anything."

CHAPTER 43

Sasha had driven, since he knew these back roads best, coming in late in the day when lengthening shadows hid many things, but it wasn't dark enough that headlights were obvious for kilometers in every direction.

As before, they were dressed in blue. There was moonlight enough that they appeared as faded gray scarecrows when they walked, moving with more care this time and approaching the Legion base along a creek bed that might let them get closer to the buildings.

Or at least didn't involve walking several kilometers across an open, flat field, when there might be enemy snipers keeping watch.

As before, lights on close to the main buildings, but the runway was dark, as were many of the hangars Sasha had entered with Yuri two months ago.

Tonight, he had the Thompson in his hands, as did Ilya. And Vanya, but his job was to protect Arkadi and his American Winchester Model 70 with the 3.5 sniper PU scope, instead of the Mosin–Nagant M1891/30 the man had used during the war.

Arkadi was still deadly enough with it that the Colonel had selected him.

They made it to a spot close to where the creek crossed the fenceline into the base.

"Arkadi, you look," Sasha ordered in a whisper. "We will stay down here out of sight."

The man nodded and moved up the slope like a snake, getting to the top and peeking over.

Minutes passed in silence, which Sasha counted as a victory.

Finally, Arkadi returned.

"They are currently working in the new hangar that they built for the Wing," Arkadi said. "Many men coming and going, with the bay doors open and folks doing things. I see a few guards moving around, but none are currently patrolling the wire anywhere close."

"Walking a wide circle every hour or two?" Vanya asked.

"Perhaps, sir," Arkadi nodded. "A long hike at night, mostly as a tripwire. They are almost directly across from us right now, walking with flashlights. That was how I saw them."

"Then we have time," Sasha said, nodding to Ilya. "You two keep watch here and prepare to cover us if something happens, or rescue us, either alone or returning with the entire team, as necessary. Make sure someone gets word out."

"I have a radio in my pack," Vanya said.

"Good enough," Sasha said. "Let's go."

He moved deeper into the dark, walking upstream in the creek bed where it was deep enough to hide him. Up ahead, he could see a bridge for a truck to drive over, but not wide enough for a large aircraft.

They paused underneath. Sasha ascended to where he could hide his silhouette against a pillar and watched.

Two flashlights, walking down the far side of the runway without any apparent energy. People making noise in the Wing's hangar. A few lights on in the main barracks, but nothing more.

No reason to expect an attack tonight, since they had just taken the Flying Wing on a long test flight and been home for only a few hours.

The craft would need to be inspected. Refueled. Tweaked. Adjusted.

Readied for whatever mission the Werewolf Legion would be taking it on.

Sasha had done the math. He estimated that such a craft probably flew around five hundred and fifty to six hundred kph. New York City would require twelve to fifteen hours flight time, depending. If you wanted to do something at night, you would need to leave around midday, returning midday as well.

Assuming you came back here.

Too many men around almost made him scrub this mission. They were exactly where he needed to go, but perhaps he could get close enough to hear something.

Or was this the moment to break into the main building, when everyone was elsewhere?

Assuming that Voss was really doing something so maniacally insane as attacking America, would he tell Escarra anything? Sasha had to assume not, or they would have tried that man's security instead.

No, he had to find something here. Now.

It felt like waiting even a few days would be too long.

Slowly, he dropped back down into the creek and motioned Ilya.

They had to get closer.

Alois had truly enjoyed flying the Wing, in ways that had surprised him. He studied it now as mechanics got to work, sitting to one side with a glass of wine to celebrate the flight.

During the war, he had flown high-performance interceptors, killing a vast array of communist scum and just about every aircraft those people had chosen to send up against him.

He had never flown bombers.

It took some getting used to. Slow and somewhat methodical. Flight surfaces without a tail meant that the aircraft occasionally wanted to slide and had to be watched.

At the same time, utterly smooth. Instinctive, in ways he couldn't explain. And hadn't needed to, because Dr. Gerstenberger had been in the navigator's seat, listening and taking notes, or offering occasional suggestions on trim and power to make things fly better.

Still, it gave him hope. At this point, the only real question was whether he would destroy the Statute of Liberty in the southern harbor, or the Empire State Building. Both were powerful symbols of the America that had thwarted his Führer and caused the fall of the Third Reich.

Damn those Japanese for everything. Had they stayed away from the Americans, Britain and Russia might have entirely fallen, and then the Japanese Empire could have easily claimed their half of the Pacific Ocean.

Now, everything was undone.

The Statue of Liberty would have to die. Simple as that. Perhaps he could find a base further north. Somewhere in the Caribbean Ocean, where he could take off at night and fly a round-trip mission to hit some other target along the Eastern Seaboard. He would have several options before the Americans caught wise and sent out aggressive patrols from their colony in Cuba.

Tomorrow's problem.

He turned to Gerstenberger, currently doing extensive calculations on several pieces of paper.

"Well, Doctor, how are we?" Alois asked.

"Normally, the aircraft could carry a full load of around seven thousand, two hundred kilograms of bombs," the scientist replied. "That's a short bombing raid, though. Buenos Aires, or someplace within a reasonable flight from here."

"We are going a bit farther," Alois reminded him.

"Indeed," Gerstenberger nodded. "Based on this test flight, we can carry safely about fifteen hundred kilograms of bombs, which is far less, but should be sufficient. It also allows us to install a pair of internal fuel tanks that ensure we can make it back to base safely with a flight reserve. Like you, I have no interest in having to land in Brazil or Venezuela, when the Americans might be able to have us arrested."

Alois nodded.

"What do you need first?" Alois asked.

Gerstenberger completed his calculation.

"Let us mount the fuel tanks first, then plumb them into place," he said. "I will calculate the bomb load and distribution that works best."

Alois turned to Sigmar and nodded. Wolf-2 began gesturing mechanics into motion. They had built the tanks, two kinds, in fact, with external drop tanks as well as internal, but he didn't know what the extra drag would do, so having fewer bombs and a solid expectation was better.

At least today. Maybe he would find a way to build an aircraft carrier or something, where he could land. Or look into the means of aerial refueling that folks were attempting.

Anything to give him greater range.

Alois would love nothing more than to annihilate the Kremlin someday.

He rose and smiled, then paused and turned back to Gerstenberger.

"Could you be ready to go tomorrow?" he asked.

That damnable Russian kept pulling lucky rabbits out of hats. Alois felt the need to get ahead of him, once and for all.

And stay that way.

"I could," Gerstenberger replied after a pause. "If they can get everything installed and the bombs loaded, I could easily sleep on the flight. You will need to be sharp, so I suggest you and your Co-pilot/Bombardier get a good night's sleep, because you will be busy for more than twenty-four hours in the air."

"Ekkehardt," Alois called. "You and I will retire. Let the others prep the Wing."

"What about the base, Alois?" Sigmar asked as Alois rose. "Should we go to alert right now, just in case?"

Alois considered it. Considered the Russian's luck, time and again.

"Yes, Sigmar," he replied. "Do that."

Not that it would matter, because he was going to strike a blow for the fallen Third Reich, but he could see teaching the Russians next.

He owed them.

CHAPTER 45

Vanya cursed quietly as every single light on the enemy base lit up.

Then he was surprised when no air raid alarms followed. No bodies exploding into motion, racing towards their jets.

"What does it mean?" Arkadi asked, still watching the base through his scope.

Vanya got just enough of his head above the edge of the creek to see. Guards continued their patrol, now down along the base of the runway and soon headed this direction, but still walking. He looked the other way and saw more guards, but they were headed away. Armed, but not rushing into battle.

"I think someone just raised the alert status," Vanya said.

"They are not acting like they saw anything," Arkadi offered. "Or that an attack is imminent."

Vanya considered things. Methodically, as he did. Logically.

What were the circumstances?

Lights on, but no panic. People moving back and forth between the big hangar and the office building where Sasha had thought the important officers would bunk. Much activity around the Flying Wing, but no other aircraft.

Sasha and Ilya had vanished up the creek bed, though Vanya could not see them now so he didn't know where they were.

Last time, the Legion had scrambled a pair of jets. Nothing like that was happening.

"It is defensive, Arkadi," he finally said.

"Sir?"

"They are going to launch an attack," Vanya deduced. "The test flight was successful, but they are not waiting around, so they have decided to prepare the Wing for an actual attack."

"And the Blackhawks?"

"Short range interceptors, Arkadi," Vanya replied. "They can escort it on take-off, and for a short time afterwards, but it must fly a considerable distance alone. They are preparing it. Later, we will see preparations for other aircraft, and that will tell us how big their target is."

"What do we do in the meantime?" Arkadi asked.

"We watch and wait," Vanya replied. "Sasha is in there and may need help escaping later. That will be our job, once we know what he plans."

At least he hoped so.

How would Sasha get out of this mess?

CHAPTER 46

Sasha had nearly panicked when the base lit up like daylight.

However, no sound followed. No threats. No gunfire.

Just day bright everywhere, which would make things all the more difficult, since their blue uniforms would stand out even more against things than the reddish brown uniforms he could see moving around.

Vanya had called the color gingerbread, and Sasha was certain now who it was that had attempted to assassinate him in town.

Not that he could return the favor at this moment.

Fortunately, they had made it as far as that farthest-out hangar, where the four Thunderbolts were stored. Not being flown as much, because the Legion had their Blackhawks now, so hopefully no reason to come inspect these aircraft in the late evening.

Still, he and Ilya were trapped at the moment. He slid quickly along the wall, then opened the door and slipped in.

"Watch the door," he ordered, even as Sasha made a quick sweep of the building. Four aircraft, no people. All he really cared about. Main doors, closed, plus the side door for people.

Not much to defend, if someone was coming for them.

Trapped, like rats.

He returned to where his navigator watched.

"Anything?" Sasha asked.

"No, which is strange," Ilya replied. "Another patrol departed, but most of the activity is in the main hangar with the wing. A few men just walked back to the main building, but nobody seems excited. What's going on?"

"I'm not sure," Sasha said. "Nobody coming this way?"

"Nobody," Ilya nodded. "One patrol is almost behind us now, still walking. One more just set out across the field. Nobody close. How do we escape?"

"We can always steal a pair of Thunderbolts if we have to," Sasha grinned. "Except that they would definitely come after us in jets if we did that, and they have radar as night-fighters. A distraction would be nice, but I presume that they will be manning anti-aircraft guns if they are on some sort of alert."

"Blow something up?" Ilya asked with a bright smile.

Sasha started to retort, then caught himself. If the Werewolf Legion was about to do something big and extravagant, maybe he needed to step up his war with them?

They'd shot at him in Buenos Aires. The uniforms matched what he remembered. And someone had sabotaged his plane and the Camel, so they were absolutely playing rough.

How rough did he wish to return unto them?

Sasha looked around and saw a mechanic's jumpsuit resting on a workbench. It gave him an idea.

He moved off, with Ilya watching, and found a second. Putting one on, he handed his partner the other.

"At least this way, we are less obvious from a distance," he said. "We will sling the machine guns and rely on pistols, so transfer your holster outside."

Suitably equipped, Sasha took a deep breath and opened the door wider, not seeing anyone immediately in sight. Quickly, he and Ilya made their way to the next hangar, where he remembered an old Martin B-10 bomber. The Americans had built them in vast numbers in the Thirties, before moving up to more impressive aircraft. Not fast or particularly effective against modern aircraft, so Sasha assumed that it was some sort of personnel transport.

If he ever established a permanent base somewhere, he might need something similar, but that was tomorrow's problem.

They slipped inside and found nobody about. It was reasonably dark in here, but the hangar doors themselves were open, admitting light, so he had to move carefully.

He went ahead and climbed inside to inspect the old craft. Fully fueled. Armed, but with American thirty caliber machine guns that were vastly outdated. Indeed passenger equipped, with six seats instead of a bomb bay.

He exited and found Ilya watching the exterior from next to the open barn door.

"Very busy around the Flying Wing, sir," Ilya noted. "Everyone is working on the bomb bay it seems, moving bombs around and a fuel truck."

"Then they are definitely going to attack someone and we must stop them," Sasha replied. "But we need to discern who they are threatening."

"I think we can slip close enough to the main building," Ilya said. "Along the fronts of the other hangars if we're careful, but for the last one, then across a courtyard and in."

"You lead," Sasha decided. "I will walk beside you."

They had pistols holstered, but he went ahead and unsnapped the flap, just in case. Ilya did the same with a nod, then took a breath and started walking directly across the space. Sasha stayed with him.

"It we look like we're talking, we'll raise less suspicion, sir," Ilya offered as they moved.

"I agree," Sasha said. "What might we be able to do in the way of distractions, were we in a hurry to leave later?"

"I remember some fuel barrels in with the Thunderbolts," Ilya replied. "The bombs all appear to be stored in a bunker well across the field where we can't get to them. And I presume they are locked and secured, though I doubt that anyone is guarding them most of the time."

"Would it be open, if they were retrieving bombs?" Sasha asked.

"It might be," Ilya nodded. "There is a truck in with the Wing that they are offloading things from with a crane. I don't know if they got the right load the first time, or will need to return for more or to return leftovers."

Sasha nodded. He hadn't worked with bombs that much during the war, except towards the end. Mostly, ferrying empty aircraft up from Persia. Or training others.

Bombs sort of magically appeared on his wings. But he'd come to appreciate Ilya's expertise with them, among other explosives.

"What if we can't stop them from taking off later?" Ilya asked.

"That aircraft is not all that fast," Sasha answered, going back to the plans he'd read about. "Half the speed of the Nightvipers, so we can always run them down if we have to. It's the Blackhawks that concern me, as they outnumber us."

"Should we sabotage some of them before we leave?" Ilya asked.

"If we have time," Sasha shrugged. "Most important is getting out with the information we need. Second is stopping the wing from doing whatever they are after. Stopping the Legion is third."

They kept walking, but now were at the gap. A courtyard paved over, with a couple of civilian automobiles and a panel truck. If he thought he could bluff his way out, he'd steal something like that and flee, but he'd seen the armed guards at the front gate. And if they were on alert, they might decide to open fire as he drove past them, then give chase.

Ilya led them across the parking lot, and up a few steps to a door. Thankfully, nobody was at the door or crossing their path, so they were able to get in easily.

Inside, Sasha took point. He had no idea how the building

might be laid out, but neither did Ilya, and he was willing to trust his luck.

Entry space like an office for a secretary, with two offices off behind it and a hallway that continued on. Sasha moved to the first office and stepped in, gesturing Ilya with him and closing the door. If was dark, so he risked a flashlight, hoping that it wouldn't be as obvious from outside as simply turning on the overhead light.

Desk and chair. Plant. Sideboard with a whiskey service. Tea service. Nothing interesting.

He moved to the door and peeked, then slipped out and into the one immediately next to it, again closing the door. No window in here, so he turned on the light and looked around.

Many file cabinets, as well as a map cabinet. On the big table, set like like an architect would use it, was a map of the Americas, both North and South, along with calipers and rulers. Sasha moved to lean over it, noting that New York City was circled with a grease pencil. Papers nearby ran calculations, and several more had a variety of weather forecasts that he understood from the war.

Definitely bombing New York City, and doing so in the next few days, from the way the forecasts were assembled and synthesized. Calm weather over the city, with a high cloud deck that would force the aircraft down low to bomb accurately.

If nobody had any warning ahead of time, the most that might happen would be that radar installations would see a single aircraft on an unannounced cargo run. If they could get far enough out to sea afterwards, they might flee entirely and never get caught.

He couldn't allow it, even if the Americans had taken it upon themselves to become his enemy.

As the Colonel had said, some evils could not be allowed to exist, and this was one of them.

Sasha nodded to himself and turned to Ilya to explain, when

the door burst inward and several armed men stood there, guns pointing in.

"What do we have here?" the one in front asked.

CHAPTER 47

Vanya was down out of sight, watching their rear as the one patrol crossed a small pedestrian bridge down a hundred and fifty meters. It was dark in his crease, but he wanted to be certain.

They crossed and kept going, passing out of sight unless he wanted to crawl to the far back. Or stick his head up as Arkadi had done.

They were alone.

"Status?" he asked just loud enough for his sniper to hear.

"Sasha and Ilya are moving towards the main building, dressed as mechanics," Arkadi replied. "I presume an infiltration. Most of the people are still focused on the wing."

Vanya nodded. So much risk. He wasn't sure why Sasha was tempting fate, save that he also had to admit to an illogical concern. An intuition that things had already spiraled out of control and they might not be able to get the aircraft under control again.

When did they bail out and try to parachute to safety? Even behind enemy lines?

Vanya didn't know.

"Sir, we have a problem," Arkadi hissed.

Vanya scrambled up and watched a group of armed men jogging towards the main building.

"What?" he asked.

"One of them saw something," Arkadi said. "Pantomime, he moved to the big one and told him. That one grabbed several others, armed themselves, and suddenly took off, ignoring most of the mechanics. All look like officers from the way they dress."

"Werewolf Legion pilots," Vanya noted. "Someone smelled trouble. You keep watch. Sasha just ran out of time and needs to be rescued."

"Sir, I can hit targets from here," Arkadi offered.

"Not you," Vanya said. "This must be bigger. Stand by and let me know if you see Sasha."

He slipped back down the bank and pulled out his bag, removing the radio and telescoping the antenna.

"This is *Ecne*, calling *Dunatis*," Vanya said, using Yuri Datsyuk's new callsign. "*Ecne*, calling *Dunatis*."

Even if someone happened to be on this channel, they would have a hard time understanding. At least Vanya hoped so.

"Go ahead, *Ecne*," Yuri's booming voice came back.

"The worst has happened," Vanya said. "I need a massive distraction here at the target."

"Understood, *Ecne*," Yuri replied. "Stand by for chaos."

Vanya had no idea what form it might take, but if Sasha was about to be captured, he would need a distraction.

Hopefully, it would come in time.

CHAPTER 48

Sasha cursed himself inwardly, but there was nothing he could do about a half-dozen men with guns pointed at him.

"Hands up," the leader snapped, a red headed man with his hair slicked back. Recognition dawned. "You are Kryvenko."

Sasha nodded, hands going up. Hopefully, someone could rescue him and he wasn't about to be shot.

"Up against the wall while we disarm you," the man ordered.

Sasha and Ilya complied as a tiny blond man slipped in and claimed both pistols and Thompsons.

"This way," the man ordered. "Wolf-6 and Wolf-8 remain. The rest of you, back to work."

Into the larger space, where they were placed against an outside wall.

"I am Alois Voss," the redhead introduced himself. "These are my werewolves. What are you doing here this time, Kryvenko?"

"You've tried to kill me several times, Voss," Sasha smiled. "I wanted to know why. Slipping in while you were busy with your new toy seemed like a good time. Going to bomb the Americans?"

"I owe them so very much," Voss replied. "The Führer had intended it, but never got the chance. I will see it done in his name."

"The war is over, Voss," Sasha told him. "The Nazi War Machine smashed. You could return to being a civilian and build a new life."

"Never, you communist scum," Voss snarled. "Your kind should have been wiped out. Pushed into the Pacific Ocean and left to drown."

Sasha bit his tongue. At least he knew where he was with this man. And had found possibly his first war criminal, if Voss was intent on continuing his Third Reich terror campaign.

"What will the Americans do to Argentina when they figure out it was you?" Sasha asked, mostly to keep the man talking. The blond and two others kept watch, but the rest had returned to the main hangar. Four on two, them armed, wasn't odds he fancied, but he did have Vanya and Arkadi outside, where hopefully they remained undetected and could do something.

What, he had no idea.

"They will not," Voss snapped. "We will hit and then slip out to sea before circling home from below their radar. It will be as if angry ghosts saw fit to set fire to the city."

Sasha nodded. It made a certain amount of sense. Radar could only see things out to a certain range before the curvature of the earth interfered.

He started to say something, when a sound caught his ear. Sasha found his head cocked as he strove to identify it.

"What?" Voss demanded, possibly hearing it as well, but not certain what it implied.

"Down!" Sasha yelled to Ilya as the sound changed pitch.

Then the world ended.

CHAPTER 49

Lyuba had kept her engines powered down to a slow efficient burn, circling the base at a fairly low altitude as she waited for…

Something.

Anything.

"*Banshee*, this is *Dunatis*," Yuri's voice came over the line.

"*Banshee*," she replied.

This.

"Proceed to target alpha and engage at low altitude," he ordered.

Technically, she outranked Yuri, both as a Captain and as Red-3 to his Red-5, but he had taken operational command, with Vanya and Sasha in the field, and her aloft.

"Confirming, *Dunatis*," she replied. "Alpha and engage."

"If you could, I'd have you do it with the engines off, Witch," he laughed. "Do the best you can."

Lyuba smiled as she checked the compass and came around.

"Three-Oh-Five," Yanina said simply. "Drop unto the deck and accelerate. I will let you know when to slow to bombing speed."

Lyuba nodded, hands working tiller and throttle as Red-3 fell out of the sky and began racing barely above the treetops.

Sasha had drawn her a map of the facility, augmented by photographs taken from a high, slanting angle.

Two anti-aircraft batteries. 20Mm Oerlikon cannon like the Americans used on warships. Both atop the main building, on opposite corners where they could cover the entire engagement hemisphere against any aircraft, and possibly any armored vehicles approaching the wire.

She'd have loved to bomb the main building, but would probably kill too many innocents doing that. Plus, she had something better in mind.

The darkness embraced her and Yanina as she raced forward.

"A little more right," Yanina said after a bit. "Yes, there. Hold that. We're in line with the air cannon and passing over one of the hangars holding Blackhawk jets. You will bomb the hangar and strafe the building to engage the cannons defending, then accelerate up and out with a clockwise orbit, before coming in on the second bombing pass. For the third pass, we will be in communications with a ground controller. Questions?"

"Negative," Lyuba laughed. "Time to raise hell."

"Just like the old days," Yanina laughed back. "But we will need someone to build us an old Polikarpov like we had at the beginning if we wish to do it right."

"Talk to Yuri about that," Lyuba smiled. "Get him on your side before we go after Sasha and Vanya."

They could probably build something remarkably similar these days, if none of the old ones still existed. Break it down for storage and carry it with them, so she could come in like the Night Witch she was, surprising the hell out of people before bombing them from utter silence in the dead of night.

"Ten seconds to contact," Yanina called. "Decelerate to bombing speed, then prepare to accelerate out the back."

Lyuba nodded and backed off the throttle. The base was an obvious target, but they were coming in low, though louder than she liked.

No tracer fire, so she had no idea if they'd seen her or not. Were shooting at her.

Still, perfectly straight and level as she lined up those two batteries, dipped her nose, and cut loose with her three 23mm NR-23 cannon, a phosphorescent chain of red glow impacting the one, then the other defensive batteries.

"Drop first bomb now," Yanina said calmly.

"Bombs away," Lyuba replied as she thumbed the switch, then opened her throttle and pulled up.

The light Nightviper howled like her own personal Irish demoness as she roared up into the night.

Behind her, an explosion as her first bomb slammed into one of the hangars, detonating a moment later in a ball of orange fire that lit the night.

Lyuba rolled as she climbed, flipping onto one wingtip and circling back down. Tongues of flame on the ground indicated men with weapons shooting at her, but only one of the guns on the roof was active, slewing around and firing his tracers at her as she started down on him.

They exchanged fire, but she was in darkness, a gray owl swooping out of the night, while he was standing in the middle of a lit building, and an illuminated air base.

Lyuba centered and watched the cannon explode under her guns, then nosed up and over to her left.

"Second bomb now," Yanina called.

Lyuba dropped it and raced away a second time as the other hangar on the end erupted in flames. That should greatly limit the ability of the Legion to challenge the Red Branch in the air, if she'd just killed half of their air force.

She stayed low to the end of the runway, running deeper into the darkness before she came back for her third run.

CHAPTER 50

Sasha heard the roar of cannon fire, then the building shook as a bomb went off just outside the window, shattering glass. Part of a wall collapsed, but onto Voss and his men, giving him an opening.

"Go!" he pulled Ilya to his feet and shoved him towards the window.

Ilya took only a moment, then dove through, with Sasha on his heels.

"Where?" Ilya asked.

Sasha looked at the closest hangar, which was on fire and partially collapsed inward, killing the Blackhawks within.

"Just run," Sasha yelled.

He put deed to word and put his head down.

Then a Nightviper made a second pass, dropping the other bomb as guns everywhere began shooting. Mercifully, nobody had seen then escape, it seemed.

At the same time, he couldn't easily cross several hundred meters of open space with killers around. And friendlies possibly strafing the base, now that the Oerlikons had been silenced.

He needed to get away, so Sasha ran around the back of the burning hangar, then started down the row of them. Two filled with Blackhawks, one on fire. Two empty. The Martin. And the Thunderbolts on the end, now destroyed by the second bomb.

Still, he had an idea.

"Follow me, Ilya," Sasha yelled.

The man stayed right on his heels as Sasha turned into the space between the fourth and fifth hangars, then raced into the open barn doors to see the Martin B-10 still intact.

For however long that remained the case. Hopefully, people would see their jumpsuits and assume that they were still friendly. At least for long enough.

"Start a quick preflight from the cockpit," Sasha said as he cleared the chocks then climbed in.

Quickly, he got into the pilot's seat, strapped himself in, and found the radio controls. American, so things he was familiar with.

"*Ecne*, this is *Cernunnos*," he said, once he found the channel he wanted.

"Go ahead, *Cernunnos*," Vanya answered instantly. "I saw where you ducked in for cover."

"We will be emerging shortly and flying away," Sasha said. "Tell whoever that we are not hostile."

"*Cernunnos*, this is *Banshee*," Lyuba came back. "Copy friendly. I'll cover you."

At moments like this, Sasha occasionally wished that he was a religious man, so he could say some sort of prayer like his grandmother might have. As it was, he was the New Soviet Man, so he simply walked across controls, testing everything and then turning the engines over.

Both engines caught cleanly. Sasha would have liked to stop and thank the mechanics who had done such an exceptional job keeping the old airframe working so well, but they were his enemies.

He nodded in their direction instead and opened the throttles to drag the craft out into the open, pausing only to turn and aim the longways down the runway before opening everything.

"We're taking fire from the ground," Ilya offered nonchalantly.

"Let them," Sasha said, pulling the throttle all the way back and starting to run.

Overhead, a Nightviper swooped, a tongue of flame emerging from the nose.

Then they were past each other and Sasha focused on the end of the asphalt, coming towards him rapidly. He pulled back the stick and the little bomber leapt into the sky.

"*Banshee*, we are airborne," he said into the radio.

"Stay low and fast, *Cernunnos*," Yanina replied. "We have high cover until you get to base."

"Roger that," Sasha said.

He retracted the main landing gear, then nosed over and found the compass. They were barely five hundred feet off the deck, but the land between here and home was gently rolling, and he could get home easily enough, assuming no Blackhawks could run him down.

At full speed, he was barely moving at three hundred and forty kph.

Would it be enough?

CHAPTER 51

Vanya watched the bomber get away, and tapped Arkadi on the leg.

"Us next," he said simply, sliding back down the creek bed and watching the space ahead.

The one patrol had already passed, then started running towards the explosions. With any luck, he and Arkadi could slip by them in the darkness and make it back to the automobile.

If not, at least Sasha had gotten away safely.

And the Werewolf Legion had more important things to do than look for him.

Alois shook his head and coughed, then sneezed as the dust got to him. He found plaster dust and wood shards atop him, but nothing heavy, so he shoved it to one side and found Wolf-8 woozy, blinking too rapidly.

Probably, the man had used his hard head to break the falling wall and protect Alois.

"Come," he said, dragging the man to his feet, even as Ekkehardt and Derek crawled from under the rubble of a book case that had fallen on them. "How are you?"

"That Russian's luck bedevils me immensely, Alois," Ekke said wearily as he rose.

"I agree," Alois said as he made his way to the door.

The main hangar, directly across from the office, was a flaming ruin. All four aircraft probably junk that would need to be replaced when this was done. Men had gotten to cover and had weapons pointed at the night sky, but already he could hear the noise of that jet declining as it raced away.

"Do we pursue?" Ekkehardt asked.

"It is probably a trap to draw us up where the others are lurking to pounce on us one by one as we launch," Alois replied. "Come, let us see where Sigmar is at."

They made their way to the main hangar, mercifully undamaged. Alois would have to give the Russian that much credit. With two bombs, he could have hit the main barracks and the hangar, possibly destroying the entire Werewolf Legion in the process, given the arrangement of Alois' troops at that moment.

Instead, the antique Thunderbolts were probably gone, along with half his Blackhawks.

"Casualties?" he asked as they found Wolf-2 covering the night with his battle rifle.

"Only a few on the ground," Sigmar replied. "Both air batteries are silent, but I haven't sent anyone up to investigate if they are all dead. All eight of us appear fine."

"I may need medical attention before I fly," Wolf-8 said quietly. "Blow to the head. Risk in high-speed maneuvering."

Alois nodded. During the war, they'd have bulled ahead and damned the consequences, but today he had made it clear to these men that they were mercenaries. That their ability to fly was the single most important thing about them.

Trying to duel someone while fighting a concussion was a good way to crash.

Plus, he'd already lost four airframes, so there was no way to send all of his wolves into battle.

"How is the Wing?" Alois asked.

"Unbothered," Sigmar replied. "Surprising, actually."

"The Russian isn't intending to fight an open war with us," Alois said. "Or wasn't. I suspect that he has changed his mind by now."

"And he stole the Martin to escape, but we were too busy dealing with the jet to stop him."

"Add it to the bill of lading," Alois nodded. "Let us talk to the Doctor about his wing, then contact our other friend. And make sure someone is manning the radar, in case they decide to come back for more."

CHAPTER 53

Sasha brought the old bomber to a rest under the heavy guns of General Navarro y Garcia's base. Hopefully, those old German cannon would be enough to convince the new Germans to stay away, though he could see adding one of those lovely American Quad-50 Halftracks at some point.

There was a plethora of old war machines about, and most folks didn't care if you paid cash for them. He would have a chat with the General when he could.

Behind him, *Banshee* was landing. She did so with consummate grace, like she did many things. It brought a smile to his face.

He and Ilya climbed out and Yuri met them at the bottom of the ladder.

"What news?" Sasha asked.

Overhead, the first hints of daylight were starting to redden the dark horizon.

"Nothing on radar that we can see," Yuri replied. "However, we're over one hundred kilometers away, so if they stayed as low as Red-3, they could get close. I alerted the gun teams, but kept everyone else grounded. *Ecne* is on his way home, supposedly driving like a madman, so I expect him soon."

"Excellent," Sasha replied. "Let us gather everyone while we await Vanya and Arkadi. And have the canteen start making coffee and food, because I suspect that we'll be up all day as well."

Lyuba taxied to her parking spot and killed her engines. He watched her hop out and appreciated her all the more for saving his life.

Sasha had had some concerns about a woman piloting team, tucked in with so many men, but Yanina had held her own with the ones she called farm-boys, and Lyuba had just reminded everyone in the world what the 46th Guards Night Bomber Aviation Regiment meant when it came to flying dangerous missions.

The *Night Witches* themselves.

He walked that way and she surprised him with a hug and a fierce kiss.

"You need to be more careful," she murmured in his ear as she stepped back.

"Acknowledged," he nodded, catching Yanina's grin as they all fell in and headed the other direction.

Pavel's face was sour, but he'd been held back at base in the ready aircraft while everyone else had been in the field.

"Your turn will come," Sasha said as he walked near the man, everyone following.

They made their way to the main building and into the dining hall that often doubled as briefing auditorium.

He turned to Yuri as folks got coffee and tea.

"*Ecne*?" he asked.

"Fifteen minutes out," Yuri replied.

Sasha checked his watch and nodded.

"Food, cigarettes, and a quick break, so I only have to explain once," he decided.

He didn't think Voss could get his bomber ready too quickly, given where they'd been before the attack.

But he knew in his soul that it was coming.

And nobody but the Red Branch would be able to stop him.

CHAPTER 54

Alois grumbled, but the mechanics were making better time than Gerstenberger had expected, so he kept his complaints inside. The tanks had been installed, tested, and fueled. The last of the bombs was rolling across the floor under expert, careful care.

Outside, the fires were out and the crews fighting them were slowly hunting down hot spots. Always a risk with fully fueled aircraft that had cannon ammunition aboard.

One of the Blackhawks had miraculously not been badly damaged, sheltered behind another that had taken the brunt of the explosion, but he would have to pull all the wreckage out and inspect the craft before it flew.

Still, that would leave him with five. Four he could send up today.

"You are still insistent?" Gerstenberger asked.

"At the minimum, Kryvenko will tell someone our plans," Alois replied. "That will get around and the locals will stop us. Arrest us, perhaps, for whatever reasons they might find. If we wish to do this thing, we must do it now. Otherwise, we likely never get another opportunity."

"There are other weapons I could design and build," the Doctor replied. "There were many significant advances, towards the end. Most failed because we simply lacked the materials to build them, with American and Russian bombers striking around the clock and destroying our factories."

"Tomorrow's problem, Doctor," Alois said. "And I will hold you to it, because I expect that this Wing will only fly once more before we have to abandon it somewhere. I will strike the Americans and hurt them. Then the Russians. And the Argentinians if they get in my way. Everyone who tries to thwart me."

"In that case, let us complete this task," Gerstenberger said. "You go brief your pilots on their tasks."

Alois nodded.

One more surprise, then he could go bomb Manhattan and avenge his Führer.

CHAPTER 55

Sasha studied the faces around him. Then noted the look on Yuri's face.

"A bomber has no business in a dogfight," he said simply.

"This camel has a scorpion's tail," Yuri replied. "I can defend myself and it flies quite well. Plus, you will need an air controller keeping watch. And anyone coming after me isn't threatening you, Sasha."

Stubborn. Like all of them.

Worse, he was probably right. The Camel was a bomber configured more as a transport, but it also had a better radar system than the Nightvipers. And guns fore and aft that would let it protect itself on a flank.

Assuming things went down as he expected.

They had all changed into flight gear in the break. Vanya was pulling his on and sipping coffee.

"The Werewolf Legion intends to bomb New York City," he began simply. "There are other targets they could hit, but this harks back to the Amerikabomber project Hitler and Goering envisioned."

"Why not Washington?" Lyuba asked.

"I see it as Leningrad and Moscow," Sasha replied. "One, an

economic center that is famous. Beyond the Kremlin itself, there are not many socially important targets in Moscow."

Nods. It made little sense, until you considered that most people thought of New York when they dreamed of America.

"How soon?" Yuri asked.

Vanya raised a hand, then pointed to Arkadi.

"I watched them install internal fuel tanks," the sniper said. "There were also several bombs on carts when Red-3 made her run, though she avoided that building."

"Perhaps I shouldn't have," *Banshee* muttered.

"No, you did the right thing," Sasha said. "We didn't know at that point what he planned, so random, mass casualties were not called for. Next time, I might change my mind, but I prefer when we work with surgical precision than act like those callous, Nazi monsters. Keep that in mind."

"How do we stop them?" Pavel asked.

"Red-3 destroyed half of his Blackhawks, I think," Sasha replied. "We will assemble in the air above our base, then set out to intercept them when they launch the wing."

"All the more reason you need me airborne, Sasha," Yuri pointed out.

Sasha nodded. All of them were aggressive. And the mission called for it. Plus, the Camel had the ability to stay in the air far longer than the Nightvipers, so he could get aloft and watch, scrambling the rest of them when it came time.

"Agreed," Sasha said. "You will launch now."

"I will go with him as escort," Vanya spoke up. "Someone needs to be in the air if those wolves come hunting. The rest of you can sit here with your fuel tanks full. If I run out of fuel, you'll have to take them down yourselves."

Sasha considered his options. All bad, but also all good.

It would take Voss time to launch. And if he only had four interceptors and a bomber, then things were actually balanced.

A fitting duel, though he didn't consider Voss a gentleman, like German pilots had acted during the First War. No, he was another Nazi punk, intent on fighting some bizarre guerrilla action long after the Third Reich had fallen.

Assuming the man didn't see himself as the harbinger of a Fourth. There were always rumors that Hitler had escaped justice, though the Americans had hauled a few of the most prominent villains to Nuremberg.

Those that they hadn't simply kidnapped and taken back to America to work on their projects, intent on stopping communism next.

And they had all been allies at one point.

"Are all the aircraft ready?" he asked the room.

"Red-3 is being refueled and reloaded," Yuri replied. "No bombs this time, and I have instructed the ground crews to attach our drop tanks instead, in order to extend our flight time, in case we need to pursue them."

"Sound logic," Sasha decided. "You and *Ecne* get aloft now and find out what they are doing. If you see Blackhawks start launching, sound the horn for the rest of us to join you. Dismissed. And good luck hunting."

They scattered, leaving Sasha alone for a long moment. Ilya would see Red-1 prepped, and the ground crews the General had provided were excellent. Good enough that Sasha had decided to start hiring some of those men permanently into the Red Branch if the old man would allow it.

Tomorrow's problem. Today, he had to save the world.

Sasha gave everyone several minutes head start. Quickly, he watched the Camel take off out a window, with Vanya close on his heels like a hound after a bear.

Modern radar made it impossible to hide, though Sasha supposed that someone would invent a device that let an aircraft disappear from radar scopes, though he had no idea how.

Merely that someone would figure out a way.

He slipped into the kitchen and grabbed a pair of sweet rolls to carry aloft. Ilya had had just as long a day, they would both need the fuel later.

"Sasha," Pavel called, chasing after him. "A minute?"

Sasha nodded and turned back. They were in the main hangar, attached to the barracks. Nobody was around, with the aircraft all out on the tarmac, but the ground crews generally kept to themselves in a separate building. And they'd been up all night according to Yuri, preparing for whatever happened.

Sasha smiled at Pavel as the man stepped close, then realized that Red-4 had his pistol in hand.

Pointed at him.

"I'm sorry, commander," Pavel said softly. "I had hoped it wouldn't come to this, but I cannot allow you to take off."

Sasha almost dropped the rolls in his surprise. Would have gone for a quickdraw, but his Shanxi was back with Voss, where it had been taken from him when they'd been captured.

"Pavel, what is the meaning of this?" he demanded, noting that the hammer was back and the barrel zeroed on his heart.

"We are not in the Soviet Union anymore, Sasha," Pavel explained ruefully. "I know that you intend to fight evil and hunt old Nazis, but that's a losing cause. I would much rather make a lot of money."

"So you've betrayed us?" Sasha asked.

"They offered me enough to live like a king, Sasha," Pavel nodded, smiling with the terrible greed that seemingly drove him. "All they asked was that you be removed from the scene, so that the Red Branch either collapsed, or perhaps got taken over by people with enough money to use us correctly."

"You're the one who sabotaged the planes?" Sasha pressed.

"And told them where to find you in Buenos Aires," Pavel nodded again. "I am utterly amazed at how many traps you have escaped, Kryvenko. But you won't get away this time."

And then a shot rang out.

PART SEVEN

DOGFIGHT

Alois had the Flying Wing out in the first light of morning. Smoke from destroyed hangars still hung over everything, but he needed to get aloft and gone before Escarra or anyone else figured out his plans and did whatever they thought might thwart him.

Nothing was allowed to stop him.

Ekke flew in the Co-pilot seat, with Dr. Gerstenberger as Navigator. Sigmar and Wolfs 4, 5, and 6—Ulrich Meyer, Friedrich Becker, and Derek Hoffmann—would fly escort for as long as they could. This version of the Blackhawk had a maximum range of about sixteen hundred kilometers. Almost exactly one thousand English miles.

However, they also had to return to this base, so there were limits to how long they could escort him as he made his run north. The Wing had to get out of range of the Red Branch, then hope that the Russians couldn't contact someone between here and there in time to warn them.

It helped that nobody would believe a defected Soviet pilot, however much the man might be an exile. The Americans had learned to hate his kind.

"Wolf-2, this is Wolf-1," Alois said on the radio. "You are clear for flight. We will be up right on your tail."

"Understood, Wolf-1," Sigmar replied. "Launching now."

Out the windshield, Alois watched the first two aircraft start forward with tongues of flames trailing both wings. Quickly, the other two joined them.

Alois fidgeted for the next two minutes like someone was driving burning slivers under his fingernails.

"Wolf-1, this is Wolf-2," Sigmar finally called. "Your skies are clear. There are other aircraft east of you that we are watching, but nothing that looks like a squadron preparing to attack, all the way to the ceiling."

Alois sighed briefly and wished he had a cigarette right now. That had been his fear. Another suicidal strafing run as he sat here helpless.

Instead, he pulled the throttle back and unlocked his brakes. The Flying Wing combined elements of the Horten H.XVIII with Northrop's plans for the YB-49, plus a few things Gerstenberger had quietly dreamed up while working for the Horten Brothers. Things that had never been built, because, as he had said more than once, they had come too late to save the Reich.

This one, at least, had been built. Flown.

As he eased back on the yoke, it was in the air for the third time in its life. Alois knew that it would be unlikely it saw a fourth, but as long as he killed the Empire State Building, his mission would be a success.

The Americans believed that their two vast oceans would protect them from war and invasion. Shattering that complacency was the greatest harm he could do to them today.

"Legion, this is Werewolf Command," Alois said into the radio. "Come to heading three-one-five and prepare to climb to altitude. Keep a routine watch aft as well as all flanks."

He had the extra fuel for it, so they could cut across the northern parts of Argentina and then Chile, before getting out over the Pacific Ocean and turning north to cross the Isthmus of Panama well to the west of the American Canal Zone and any American defenses.

With any luck, he would be approaching his final target in the twilight hours, instead of the middle of the night as he had intended, but in his heart, Alois knew he was only going to get one chance at this.

Here. Now. It was necessary to grasp it or fail.

The original Flying Wing design had called for a ball turret aft but he had left it off to save weight and increase his fuel. Some had included dorsal or ventral turrets as well. All had been removed in order to get the most range possible from the design.

To make a single round-trip flight to New York City and back if possible.

To effect his vengeance.

He had to rely on his wolfpack now.

CHAPTER 57

Sasha flinched, then watched Pavel topple slowly—silently—to the ground, surprise etched into the betrayer's face.

He looked up and Lyuba stood there, her own Shanxi in hand and smoking as she thumbed the safety block and dropped the hammer before kneeling to inspect the body.

Sasha was down with her. The shot had taken Pavel in the heart, but at enough of an angle as to not keep going into Sasha's chest next, though he supposed after a moment that the .45 hit slower than the 7.63mm or Red Nine it had evolved from. Might not have exited Pavel's chest.

The man was absolutely dead. Sasha grabbed his pistol and dropped the hammer. For now, he put it in his own holster.

"How did you know?" he asked her.

"He has been acting strangely," she replied. "Initially, I thought it might be jealousy, because he had tried to court me and I had politely rebuffed him. Since the incident with the aircraft, I had watched him closer, wondering if he had been our saboteur. When Vanya and Yuri took off, I held back in the shadows. And heard him admit it."

Sasha rose, drawing her to her feet. Footsteps running closer turned out to be various ground crew personnel. Sasha waved a hand at the nearest one.

"This man is dead," he said simply. "Contact the General and I will explain it all to him, but we do not have time to deal with the body at the moment."

"A priest, commander?" the man asked.

Local. Swarthy. Hispanic. Presumably Catholic.

"He was not a believer," Sasha replied. "But I do not suppose that it could hurt. We will talk when I return."

Outside, engines suddenly roared in the way of jets preparing to taxi.

He had run out of time, but Sasha grabbed Lyuba long enough for a quick kiss.

"Thank you," he said, then stepped back and started to run to his jet.

The final dance had begun.

CHAPTER 58

Yuri flew like a cargo transport, down around three thousand meters and slow enough that his controls were a little mushy, but he needed to not stand out on any of the radar systems he could pick up around him.

The Legion took off from northeast of Cordoba, but he and Red-2 had already moved further north, past the lake and on a general northwesterly heading, as if flying to Santiago del Estero or San Miguel de Tucuman.

Not a threat to the Werewolf Legion. At least until they got close enough to study him visually.

Red-2 stayed well off on his right flank, out far enough to appear separate, and well above in case he needed to swoop.

"Yuri," Dmitri drew his attention on the intercom. "I have them."

Yuri would have been surprised that the system could see that far onto a flank, but it was Dmitri. There would be ways to accomplish it.

"You are certain?" Yuri asked automatically.

"Two and two more," Dmitri nodded. "Followed by a fifth sitting in the middle of a diamond formation."

Yuri nodded. Of course.

"Oleg, let Sasha know," he said. "Oh, and arm your cannons."

Because the Camel would have to get involved before this day was done. Of that, he was dead certain.

CHAPTER 59

Vanya heard the call and trusted Dmitri had them. Currently, he was alone, but the other would be racing to his side shortly. So they were evenly matched. Four on four, and two bombers.

Would it be enough?

"*Ecne*, this is *Cernunnos*," Sasha said over the radio. "Red-4 is grounded. Repeat, Red-4 is grounded."

WHAT?

Vanya had so many questions, but Sasha's matter-of-fact tones disinclined him to ask over an open channel.

"Acknowledged, *Cernunnos*," he replied instead.

Glancing over at Arkadi, he got a shrug from the man.

Three on four, then. They would have to make it count.

"*Cernunnos*, this is Red-5," Dmitri called a few minutes later. "What is your status?"

"Closing at maximum speed, *Dunatis*," Sasha replied. "Four minutes to contact."

"Roger that," Dmitri called.

Vanya watched the radar return.

"Red Branch elements, enemy aircraft have turned to engage," Dmitri announced. "Red-2 and Red-5, four enemy aircraft inbound."

Vanya cursed to himself and kicked his rudder hard over, snapping up on one wing as he brought his nose about.

"Arkadi, find them," he ordered, seeing a silver glint that was the Camel, about to be beset by several Nazi pilots in cutting edge American interceptors.

He was on his own until Sasha and Lyuba got here.

What had happened to Pavel? Or worse, what had Vanya missed in trying not to act like a commissar around his new comrades?

He would find out later.

Right now, he had to protect his friends.

CHAPTER 60

Yuri studied the screen as Dmitri showed four aircraft closing at more than nine hundred kph, two pairs flying in a classic wingman on wingman formation that would make it difficult to engage, especially as they were currently outnumbered.

"Red-2, this is Red-5," Yuri said calmly. "Prepare to climb."

He didn't bother waiting for a response, instead pulling the throttle all the way back in tandem with the stick.

Something Sasha had shared had caught in his mind. The Blackhawk had a rate of climb around twenty-five hundred feet per minute as the Americans measured it. The Camel could top that, though his foes would have an ever-so-slight edge in maximum service ceiling when they finally caught him.

They'd still have to catch him, first.

Four aircraft swooping and accelerating down, possibly reaching one thousand kph. Idly, as the Camel roared, he wondered if those craft could reach the mythical speed of sound, somewhere above twelve hundred.

The Camel could not. It was slower, balkier, and had a tendency to be a total pain in the ass. Just like a real camel. He'd met a few in Persia. And been spit on.

"Oleg, you engage as you can," Yuri called over the intercom. "Dmitri, where is Red-2?"

"Below you and coming up," Vanya replied. "One pass, then I will be waiting for you at altitude."

Yuri nodded. The Nightviper had a climb rate of more than nine thousand feet per minute, almost a rocket, but they had the worst ceiling as those things were measured.

Still, getting up and away would buy Sasha and Lyuba time to close. He wondered what had happened to Pavel, but someone had also tried to kill him by cutting control wires in the Camel. If it had been Pavel, best that someone else killed him before Yuri got his hands on the man.

Pavel Zaslavsky would be begging for death for a long time in that case.

"Thirty seconds," Dmitri called. "Still closing at high speed."

Yuri nodded. He was flying a pig, not a weasel.

Still, maybe this old dog had a few tricks left. If he looked at them as Panther tanks on the ground below, he was back in the cockpit of his Il-2 Sturmovik, or later, the upgraded Il-10.

Tank hunting in the swamps and fens.

Yuri laughed, then rolled onto one wing, slewed his nose around, and lined up on the second Blackhawk he could see in the distance, terrible carrion crows come to pluck out his eyeballs and feast on them.

You better kill me first, then.

The Camel had guns on both ends. Two Nudelman-Rikhter NR-23 cannons in the nose, and the other pair in a barbette that Oleg controlled aft.

He wasn't about to dogfight these fools, but for a few minutes, it would be hounds on a bear. Hopefully, they had remembered to strap on the spikes collars real bear hunters equipped their dogs with.

He could almost feel Dmitri's shrug as the closure rate jumped to something impossible, somewhere north of eighteen hundred kph. Distances measured in eyeblinks more than anything.

"Up and right just a shade," Dmitri said calmly. "Then fire a burst NOW!"

Yuri did, watching a stream of tracer rounds intersect with the craft he had been aiming at, even as the others had to hold their fire, lest they jostle too closely at high speed and touch wingtips.

One fired. He wasn't sure if they hit from the way the aircraft was already rumbling, roaring, and vibrating madly, but it didn't come apart on him and no alarms sounded.

"Climbing out!" he yelled, mostly to warn Oleg, though he felt the rear cannons speak, a dull staccato in his sternum.

Yuri stood the Camel on its hairy ass and ran like hell.

CHAPTER 61

Vanya watched that crazed Cossack initiate a cavalry charge against a line of Polish Hussars and had to laugh. He'd worried that Sasha was the emotional one, before Vanya realized that he was really the only calm, sane member of the organization, and that the others were *all* like that.

Still, it worked. Red-5 broke the formation into two wing components, pairs splitting away left and right as *Verblyud* bombed madly through their formation. Better, the tail guns had a low-deflection shot and one of the Blackhawks began to spew smoke out of one wing suddenly.

And they might have forgotten about Red-2, because both pairs began to circle around again, going after Red-5 as the bomber stretched his lead with a better climb rate. That, or the wounded aircraft and his wingman were distracted.

Vanya throttled back and slid sideways to his left, matching speed with the larger Blackhawks and studying his options. He had about two seconds to act.

Vanya lined his gunsight on the wounded one. Better a solid kill now than one that might recover later. He fired, and watched one engine nacelle suddenly explode in flames and debris, the aircraft sliding into a flat spin on one wing and the stub of the other.

As the other started a climb to escape, that pilot over there suddenly realized that the Blackhawk was outclassed, Vanya staying tight on his tail as both maneuvered, one fleeing and Red-2 trying for a second kill.

"Arkadi, watch the other pair and warn me if they break off from Red-5," he said.

"Already have them," his navigator replied. "I expect them to turn to engage with Red-1 shortly. They're close."

Vanya nodded. The man in front of him was among the best pilots Vanya had ever fought, jigging, twisting, and rolling, making a kill shot impossible so Vanya conserved his ammunition.

Instead, he stayed with the man, waiting for a mistake.

"Red-2, what is your status?" Sasha called.

"Engaged with one," Vanya replied. "Red-5 could use some help."

"Understood," Sasha said. "Engaging now."

At least the numbers were even.

Time to see how good this Nazi really was.

CHAPTER 62

Sasha finally appreciated the raw speed of the Nightviper. It lacked the pure performance of the new Mikoyan-Gurevich MiG-15 designs that he had flown as a test pilot, but had an exceptional straight-line speed when he'd needed to push things to the red line and run down Red-5.

"Red-3, stand by to jettison your drop-tanks," he said as he studied the battle.

It was risky, because he gave up range when he did that, but he needed to dogfight with unknown German pilots right now. And hopefully, the tanks wouldn't hit anyone or a cow when they hit the ground, but again, nothing he could do but hope.

"Standing by," she replied.

"Drop now," he ordered, flipping the switch and feeling his steed grow that much faster and more nimble.

The British had the most experience with jet-powered fighters, though the Germans had often built better ones. And earlier. The Argentine Air Force was taking possession of Gloster Meteors such as had flown in 1944, but those were at least a whole step less capable than the original de Havilland Vampire, to say nothing of the Venom design that had been turned into the Nightviper with a few tricks that Soviet design bureaus had quietly come up with.

What an amazing time to be alive, as the new technology seemed to leap ahead annually, for those folks who could afford to stay on the cutting edge.

How long would the Nightviper be preeminent? How soon until he needed to re-equip his team with something newer, faster, better? And what form would it take, because he knew that most straight-wing jets, including the Nightviper, couldn't tangle with the swept-wing MiG-15?

Other people were going to discover that to their dismay, but for today, he had similar aircraft facing off. Two Blackhawks that had peeled away from chasing Yuri as Sasha got close, though they'd kept their distance once Oleg had opened fire.

You had to be flanking a bomber with turrets, cutting across their formation when they couldn't maneuver to engage you, like the mighty swarms he had escorted to Berlin at the end.

"Red-3, stay tight," he ordered.

"Watching your back," Lyuba replied.

She was good. He had wondered why the Colonel had included her. Now he knew. Low-level bombing precision better than his. And exceptional skills at altitude.

What did the Germans have?

"Accelerating," Sasha said, opening his throttle that last notch.

Both Blackhawks had slowed while climbing. Now, they were nosed over and diving away from him, speeding up.

The Nightviper simply had better engines, variants of the Klimov VK-1 that powered the MiG-15, instead of the older de Havilland Ghost 103. More power. More importantly, more speed.

They began to swoop away, still back-footed as the British might call it, by his arrival. And the surprise that the Camel had a scorpion tail.

"Red-5, maintain contact with our main target," Sasha reminded him. "Do not engage at present, but don't let him get away in this mess."

"Understood, Sasha," Dmitri replied.

Though, he supposed, they could go hunting, as the Camel was armed, too.

Hopefully, it wouldn't come to that.

He started his chase.

CHAPTER 63

Lyuba felt more alive when she was flying to kill. There was simply nothing else that came close save taking a good lover to bed. Like Sasha. Exceptional on both counts.

"Yanina, keep an eye on Vanya, in case he gets in trouble," she ordered.

"Understood," her sidekick wench said simply.

The Nazis were trying to run away. And failing. Shortly, they would snap around to fight, but what she couldn't guess was if they would come about as a pair, or split to force her and Sasha to ignore one or also split to follow.

And there they went, each headed a different direction.

"Sasha, I have the wingman," Lyuba called, standing her little stallion on one wing to cut the chord on that Blackhawk.

"Understood, Red-3," he replied. "I have the leader."

She'd never flown anything more sophisticated than the old Polikarpov Po-2/U-2LNB until after the war, when a few women had been allowed to remain air force pilots. And discover jets. All those nights of wishing she'd had something faster and more powerful, when they'd been hunted down by the Messerschmitt Bf 109 and Focke-Wulf Fw 190 fighters.

The only thing that had usually saved them back then was that those aircraft couldn't slow down enough to engage at low altitude without stalling and crashing. Usually. Sometimes, they got lucky.

Today, she had a better jet than those Nazi bastards who had killed so many of her sisters in battle. Lyuba was about to make the most of it.

Her target flew a circle, but she was inside his turn radius, cutting across and firing before he realized that she had moved with him. Quick reactions on the German's part got his nose up and his speed cut way back, almost forcing a stall but turning him away before he flew into her cannon rounds.

Then he tried to stall it and force her to overfly him, switching places in battle. A lesser pilot might have fallen for it, but she turned back against him, cutting her engine back as well, then slipping onto her left wing before sharply snapping back over to her right.

He had bought himself five seconds of safety, at the cost of her now being directly above and behind him, where she could watch his tail give him away as things moved.

And he couldn't get away from her here, so she paused for a second, pretty sure she was in his blind spot from the way that large tail was built.

Dead black aircraft, with long, thin wings. Big tail. Two nacelles that ran through the wings instead of slung underneath.

And a large aircraft, almost twice as long as her Nightviper. She felt like a shrike harrying a vulture.

Then he realized where she was, because Lyuba watched his tail pitch the nose down into a hard dive, starting a right-hand spiral to try to escape her.

Again, she rode him like a buckaroo, watching his instincts and training try to shake her off.

Finally, she fired, catching him flattening out as he went to reverse into a left-hand spiral.

Her round slammed into his tail assembly, blowing holes in his rudder and elevators that caused the craft to drift and yaw into a sideslip that didn't appear to be under control.

He lost velocity, possibly trying to regain control, so she backed off her throttle and let a little space develop between them.

Then a second burst. She caught him aft of the cockpit, about where the wing spars mated with the body. Flames erupted, so she must have gotten a fuel tank or a line.

Smoke began to pour out, blinding her for a moment, so Lyuba climbed back up above him, content for now to watch while the Nazi decided what to do next.

"Anyone threatening us?" she asked, catching Yanina turning to look over their split tail.

"Not yet," her friend replied. "Sasha and Vanya both have their foes in hand, it seems."

"Excellent," she said, turning her attention forward again.

The Nazi's cockpit canopy suddenly exploded up and away, forcing her to flare off to her right so as to not risk hitting it.

A moment later, both men in the cockpit were jettisoned into the air by what looked like formal ejection seats.

Lyuba was impressed. The Luftwaffe had built such things into aircraft like the Heinkel He-219 long before anyone else had taken such devices seriously. Here, she watched the device rocketed both men up and clear of that tall empennage, then split into two parts as she circled away from the mess.

Coming back around, two parachutes had deployed separately, both men falling but generally safely to land somewhere in the Argentinian landscape below.

Lyuba considered how the Germans might have treated a Soviet pilot in similar circumstances, but chose to fly by them at a slow enough speed that they could see her instead of opening fire, then dove after the flaming Blackhawk starting to tumble. One more burst and it detonated, pieces cast outward in all directions that would rain down on the countryside, though she didn't see any cities or even towns below.

Good enough.

"Where are the rest of them?" she asked Yanina.

CHAPTER 64

Sasha watched the two Legion fighters split, the one continuing his hard turn while the other reversed away, both accelerating.

"Sasha, I have the wingman," Red-3 said sharply.

"Understood, Red-3," Sasha replied. "I have the leader."

Watching the four original fighters charging Yuri on the radar screen as he had closed, Sasha was certain that this was the leader of the flight. What he couldn't tell was if it was Voss in the craft ahead of him, or one of his flunkies, with Voss on that bomber trying to slip away from them.

His Nightviper could outrun any of them. And he had full tanks right now, having just dropped the external, so Sasha could concentrate on his foes one at a time.

This one slewed back and forth like a sled on a toboggan run, riding up both sides before sliding back down and across too fast for Sasha to get a clean shot at him.

And he was good. Possibly good enough to win, had he not made one critical mistake at the beginning by trying to kill Yuri instead of focusing on his Nightviper foes.

Air combat was an unforgiving place. Already, Vanya had shot one of his enemies out of the sky, leaving the two sides balanced at three apiece.

Sasha had to make it work. And had the best of the four pilots right now, because the man was doing things with that Blackhawk that even the manufacturer probably didn't think it could do, trying to shake Red-1 off his tail.

Sasha stayed with him. Slid in tight and crept closer every time that pilot shifted, because the Blackhawk simply wasn't as maneuverable.

And the future would only get better, because the Soviet Union was starting to build MiG-15s in operational numbers. What would the Americans and British do to counter it?

Better, what would he be facing, the next time he had to tangle with the Werewolf Legion? Because Sasha didn't think that he could end them today, short of somehow returning to base after this mission, rearming, and bombing their hangars out of existence.

Where did personal conflict turn into the sorts of open warfare that would cause Peron's government to intercede? Or would they chase the Red Branch entirely of the country? And where would everyone end up?

Sasha didn't know. Didn't care today. He let his instincts fly the craft while the other pilot barrel-rolled up and over to his right, then continued his roll and put the craft into a hard, inverted dive.

Lyuba had mentioned that she didn't think the Nightviper could sustain Mach 1.0 without disintegrating. Flight tests had proven that swept wings were probably necessary. And better engines.

Still, he had to push. Had to roll with that wolf and harry him down, a mastiff growling.

They'd started at six thousand meters. Now they were both pointed almost straight down, wind buffeting his Red-1's wings and fuselage hard as they kept up their spiraling dive.

"Mach zero-point-nine," Ilya called calmly, though loud enough to intrude on Sasha's mind. "Point nine-three. Point nine-five."

Sasha was amazed. The best the Nightviper was supposed to

achieve was roughly zero-point-nine. And both of them were pushing the envelope as far as it would go right now. And he could feel his control slipping aft as the windstream around them got hectic and unpredictable.

Sasha was locked hard on the other craft, so he was able to pull out and get clear when the Blackhawk's entire tail assembly suddenly ripped off the aircraft, nearly hitting Sasha as he rolled away hard enough that his own wings were screaming in pain around him.

Sasha got out of his roll before he tried to to anything else, dialing down his power as he fought the control surfaces that wanted to slide off the wind and keep diving.

For a moment, he thought Red-1 was about to break up around him, just like that Blackhawk had done, then he fought it to submission and he got the nose up enough to point at sky instead of ground, blowing out a hard breath as he did.

"That was interesting," Ilya offered phlegmatically.

Sasha laughed. The man played with high explosives. He did everything with a degree of calm that Sasha found almost entirely alien.

A good pairing. A good team, when he looked at the other pairs and how they came together in a greater whole, though he wasn't sure what he would do with Nikon Ilyin, Pavel's navigator.

"Where are they?" he turned to the man.

CHAPTER 65

Alois wanted to scream. Rage. Something.

Wolf-2 stopped responding on the radio, and Alois knew that he was alone in the sky with his worst enemies. Four wolves, defeated in aerial combat.

Alois knew he was a better pilot than any of the others. Had he made a mistake by not flying himself and Ekkehardt in the interceptors? Ekkehardt was almost as good. Better than Sigmar had been.

He growled a terrible curse and looked up and over his shoulder.

"Wolf-3 to any Wolf units," Ekkehardt said calmly into the radio.

One more try.

Nothing.

The man shrugged.

"Can we outrun them?" Gerstenberger asked simply.

But the man knew that truth as well. The Flying Wing was exceptionally efficient, granting fantastic range. The cost was speed. And he had modern jet interceptors coming after him. There had been three. He had to assume that his mole had been discovered at the end and killed. There was no other explanation for Kryvenko being here.

He had gambled, and lost.

"Here they come," Ekke said simply.

Worst, they were still over Argentina, not even having made it over the mountains into Chile, as slow as this beast sailed.

"Doctor, we have two choices," Alois offered, as calmly as he could in spite of his white hot rage. "We can bail out here and try to escape them on the ground, or we can die in a blaze of meaningless glory when they shoot this aircraft down. I intend to aim at that collection of volcanoes on the Chilean border and set the autopilot to fly the wing into the ground. Without that, there is far less chance they can convince someone of our true plans. Or at least it buys us enough time to get out of Argentina."

"Where will we go?"

"Elsewhere," Alois snapped. "Let us survive this day and then see what we can salvage from my mistakes."

Gerstenberger nodded silently.

"Ekkehardt, you get the good doctor out the bottom hatch with an emergency bag, then see to getting him to safety."

"Will the Russians shoot us as we fall?" the man asked, already rising and gesturing.

"They will shoot us shortly when they arrive," Alois said. "At least this way, they might miss you, if you fall a bit before opening your chute."

"Until tomorrow, commander," Ekkehardt said.

Quickly, Alois was alone.

"Voss, this is Kryvenko," that damnable voice came over the radio. "Are you going to surrender?"

"No," Alois replied, after chewing on his reply for a moment, dialing back the power another notch and locking in the autopilot to hold it into a soft dive.

Those volcanic peaks were all above six thousand meters, so it was likely that the wreckage would be scattered all over inhospitable terrain.

"We will shoot you down if you do not come about and return to base, Voss," Kryvenko said simply.

Alois decided to let the man have the last word. Ekke and Gerstenberger were already gone, the thin air sucking all the oxygen and heat out of the aircraft as he hooked the last emergency bag to his parachute frame and took the two steps to where he could look down and see the green already giving way to the brown stone of the uplands.

Alois cursed his luck and the gods that had favored those communist scum, then pulled his arms in tight and stepped into eternity.

CHAPTER 66

Sasha had Red-1 on a soft glide, bucking at the slow speeds he had to maintain as he stayed above and behind that bomber.

And it was diving, however slowly. Going to slam into the mountains ahead at this rate.

Glancing right and left, he noted Vanya and Lyuba on his wings, like geese headed north for the winter.

They were above the Wing, and Sasha had a chance to appreciate the stunning beauty of the craft. Long and wide. Low and elegant, like a ray moving through calm waters.

"This is your last warning, Voss," Sasha announced. "If you do not come about, I will shoot you down."

He waited.

Nothing.

"Red-5, are there any other aircraft on an intercept path?" he asked.

Yuri had stayed well clear, turning onto something of a reciprocal course that let him point his radar at Cordoba and even Buenos Aires in the grand distance.

"Negative, Red-1," Dmitri replied quickly. "Clear skies."

Sasha nodded.

"Do we assume he is committing suicide?" Ilya asked on the intercom.

"I do not," Sasha said. "Merely getting low enough that we have to chase him. He can still climb back up if we leave him alone. It is necessary to end his threat. Places like New York City might think they are my enemy, but they must be protected nonetheless from people like Voss. They might never appreciate it, but that doesn't change the necessity of our behavior."

"Understood," Ilya acknowledged.

Hard life. As recently as three years ago, they had all been allies. Friends, even, with American factories supplying the Bell P-39 Airacobra and P-63 Kingcobra that had been so effective at first stopping the Luftwaffe, then driving them back.

The Soviet Union could not have survived otherwise.

Pity that the West had gone back to believing that communism was a greater threat to humanity than fascism.

It wouldn't change his action.

"Red Branch, stand by to engage final enemy target," Sasha said over the radio.

He was above them and back the perfect distance for his cannons. The Wing was flying perfectly steady, instead of attempting whatever maneuvers an aircraft like that might undertake to evade.

He had read where the lack of a tail often made them behave in strange and unpredictable ways, but no Soviet design bureau had gone very far in pursuing such aircraft.

Sasha nosed Red-1 over and lined up his gunsight with the right-hand engine cluster, four contrails emerging on that side. He triggered a long burst and watched flames suddenly erupt on that side, even as the engines died.

Beside him, Vanya killed the other engines.

The Wing hung for a few moments, then tipped onto one side and began to spiral, a column of smoke marking its plunge into the depths and out of the sky.

Sasha pulled back and climbed away, leading the other two clear, then circling wide to come back around and watch the machine slam into the ground, detonating as Voss must have armed all the bombs.

There would be no survivors from that.

Had Voss decided to die in battle, or slink away? No parachutes had emerged, but they could have fled earlier. At jet speeds, the ground moved by quickly. Plus, several of the Werewolves had ejected from destroyed aircraft. Even the one Sasha had been chasing had managed to get clear as it fell, so presumably remnants of the Werewolf Legion were scattered across northern Argentina.

Lyuba wasn't the only one that had shown mercy to her foes. Hopefully, it would not return later to spite them.

For now, Sasha had won. Had protected however many innocent Americans from the terror of a night strike on their most famous city.

He would let General Navarro y Garcia inform Peron's government and others what had happened up here tonight, and let them handle it. His job had been to stop Don Escarra from committing terrible acts, either by intent or having been duped by Voss.

"Red Branch, this is *Cernunnos*," he said simply as he brought the nose of his Nightviper around. "We are returning to base."

He wondered what Colonel Nazarenko would say when he heard.

CHAPTER 67

Sasha had showered and put on his best blue uniform. General Navarro y Garcia had seemingly done the same. And had asked Sasha to bring Vanya and Lyuba with him to the man's vast estate.

Vanya had muttered the word *kulak* exactly once as they traversed the long driveway, then kept to himself. Lyuba smiled like a queen.

They were in the main library on the ground floor, where there was space. The butler he knew served as bartender today. And possibly witness.

Nobody ever appreciated how much the staff and servants heard on a daily basis. And how much they gossiped. Still, Sasha had few secrets, and none that would come up today.

They drank Irish whiskey, presumably in celebration that the Red Branch was an Irish corporation. The word whiskey itself came from the Irish *uisce beatha*, meaning *water of life*.

Sasha preferred vodka, but supposed that he would learn to drink many new things, in his life as an exile.

"And from there, we flew back to our base, landed, and contacted you, General," Sasha completed his tale. "I don't know how many members of the Legion there are right now, nor what the Argentine government will do about them."

"I have let a few folks know some of the truth," the General replied. "They are properly aghast at the entire situation, and will likely ostracize Escarra for a considerable amount of time. Possibly as long as a whole month, knowing local politics."

He paused, a twinkle in his eyes at the joke. Then he raised his glass.

"To the Red Branch," the General said simply. "For things that might never be told to the wider public. And for being the kinds of heroes that this modern age needs."

They drank to that.

"What will you do next, General?" Sasha asked.

The old man shrugged.

"I had hired you to protect myself from the Werewolf Legion, as you know," he said simply. "That threat is likely neutralized, because my government contacts hinted that they would force Escarra to disavow Voss and his people. Likely, the Legion will be chased out of Argentina and told to never return. Which might last as long as a year. Or the next major crisis. I can keep you on staff for a time, but I expect the government to question having my own private air force at some point, at which time I will probably have to fire the lot of you."

"I am less worried about that outcome, sir," Sasha nodded. "If you tell a few folks what we did here, I expect that others might have similar problems requiring similar assistance."

"Would you have flown for the Chinese nationalists?" the General asked. "Before they began losing the final war against Mao?"

Sasha shrugged.

"It is hard to say," he replied diplomatically. "The American government remains keenly involved at this point, though I do not believe that the Nationalists can survive, though there are rumors of them fleeing entirely to Formosa at some point."

Sasha nodded. He had an extremely low opinion of Chiang Kai-Shek as a commander. The man seemed to be a highly charismatic dictator, but almost incompetent when organizing a military campaign. Plus, he kept firing his competent generals when they got too successful. Possibly jealousy drove him more than anything.

"You can rest assured that I will put the word out that you might be on the market soon," the General nodded. "Have you given thought to how you will replace the man who betrayed you?"

"I have not, at present," Sasha said simply. "His navigator swears that he had no idea what Zaslavsky was up to, and I tend to believe him for now. Finding a skilled jet pilot will be more complicated than merely posting a help wanted poster, as you might imagine. And I doubt that Argentina has had enough time to develop those skills, having only recently begun to fly the older Meteors. Still, many places are flying similar aircraft to our Nightvipers, so I have hope that I might find someone."

"Again, I will put out the word there, too, Sasha," he said. "Now, my friends, let us spend the afternoon telling an old pilot of your exploits, both recently as well as during the war. I have sent a messenger to your base, and a truck to bring the rest of your team here for a banquet later where we can celebrate everything, but I miss flying. I hope you will understand."

Sasha nodded. Luck had led him to Melendez and then the General, where they had been able to stop Voss, who would be permanently added to the Colonel's list of war criminals to be hunted down, once folks in Moscow were updated.

For now, he could talk about the Great Patriotic War, and how the Soviet Union had saved the world.

CHAPTER 68

Gennadi smiled as the door opened and Sasha slipped into the back room of the restaurant. He'd gotten into Argentina on a fake passport that identified him as an Irish businessman with a Russian background.

One of the Whites, perhaps, who had fled after the Civil War more than twenty-five years ago. People didn't ask closely and he generally replied with a wink and a nod.

The beard did an excellent job of hiding his face, and he had taken to wearing a Swiss-style cap that added an element of jauntiness to his day.

He rose with only a little pain and shook Sasha's hand, then got him seated.

Back room. More a storage room than anything, barely big enough for two and a waiter, but the door closed and the owner was operating under the mistaken belief that Gennadi was working for British Intelligence.

Spy games, but entirely misdirected. As they should be.

"I was surprised to get your note," Sasha said quietly.

"We do not have the means to secure communications across the Atlantic easily," Gennadi replied. "My superiors have already started falling over themselves to grant me greater flexibility in how I handle things, after your successes."

"I stopped one enemy from attacking another enemy, Genna-di," Sasha said quietly.

"You stopped what might have escalated into the next Great War, Sasha," Gennadi replied soberly. "Berlin already has things at far too high a level of stress for certain folks back home. Events in China are proceeding to their inevitable conclusion, and might trigger it there yet. Korea remains a mess that has burned out of sight of most people. Japan will want the Kurill Islands back at some point. And the Iron Curtain will make things worse. I still believe that Berlin was a mistake on our part, and the Americans called Stalin's bluff, but I do not know how they can back away gracefully, as the airlift has crystallized things for the people of western Germany and the western zones of Berlin. They have found themselves again and drawn a line in the sand."

"What next, sir?" Sasha asked.

Gennadi paused at a knock, followed by the door opening and fresh bread being delivered.

That turned into ordering, and it was several minutes before they were alone again.

"What next?" Gennadi asked. "There are rumors that Voss escaped. Possibly all of the men on that raid, depending on which checklist you follow. They are being listed on various Interpol notices as wanted and dangerous, but many nations would be willing to ignore such things, though they are probably done in Argentina. At least for now."

"What about the Red Branch?" Sasha asked. "I do not believe that you expected us to blow up as we did."

"You have become heroes to some," Gennadi nodded. "Villains to others. And generally orthogonal to our interests, but it will provide you access to places you would not have, previously. Possibly even the United States, once they digest what the Werewolf Legion intended."

"Can we still hunt war criminals effectively?"

"We'll see, Sasha," Gennadi replied. "It may be that you transform into a more public organization, and we need to add staff that can handle the quieter elements, keeping them out of the spotlight that you will come to dominate."

He watched the young man nod sagely.

"What do we do about Pavel?" he asked finally.

"I have begun to look for a replacement, but that will take time, as the four of you were head and shoulders above the rest, when it came time to select," Gennadi said. "And it was my mistake to overlook that his past black marketeering might get out of hand. I had hoped that being an old comrade of yours would mean more to the man."

"Anyone can be seduced by the right bribe, Gennadi," Sasha nodded. "The others have given me no reason to doubt their sincerity, but I watch."

"You might also bring in an outsider, if one presented themselves," Gennadi offered.

"What would I tell them about our kit?" Sasha asked.

"Britain was extremely close to remaining friends with the Soviet Union, Sasha," Gennadi reminded him. "They gave us the engines that have turned into the future of Soviet aviation. Perhaps the British quietly built russified versions of their Vampire, and you stole them. Or stole the plans and had money in Ireland that built them, which is close enough to the truth for now, as I have such a factory quietly making parts now."

"Oh?"

"Ireland has no love of the English," Gennadi pointed out with a wry smile. "Their revolution and civil war happened just before ours. As long as we are quiet, they will assist."

"Good to know, sir," Sasha said, reaching for some bread and the oil. "Will the separation into Eastern and Western Europe mean that we do not return to operate there?"

"You will go where the money takes you, Sasha," Gennadi told him solemnly. "And hunt those escaped Nazis that should be in prisons or dancing at the end of a noose. Past that, I cannot tell you what the future will bring."

"We will be ready to face it," Sasha nodded.

"I know, Sasha," Gennadi smiled. "It will be up to us to save the world, but most of that weight will fall on your shoulders. You can handle it, Atlas-like. That is why I selected you."

"I will do my best, Colonel," Sasha replied.

"That, Sasha, is all any of us can do."

READ MORE!

Be sure to pick up all the books in The Red Branch series!
https://www.knottedroadpress.com/series/the-red-branch

ABOUT THE AUTHOR

Blaze Ward writes science fiction in the Alexandria Station universe (Jessica Keller, The Science Officer, Phil Kosnett, etc.) as well as several other science fiction universes, such as Corsac Fox, Operation Marrakesh, and more. In addition, he is the Editor and Publisher of *Boundary Shock Quarterly Magazine as well as Thrill Ride Magazine* . You can find out more at his website www.blazeward.com, as well as Patreon, bluesky, Facebook, Goodreads, and other places.

Blaze's works are available as ebooks, paper, and audio, and can be found at a variety of online vendors. His newsletter comes out regularly, and you can also follow his blog on his website. He really enjoys interacting with fans, and looks forward to any and all questions—even ones about his books!

Never miss a release!
If you'd like to be notified of new releases, sign up for my newsletter.

http://www.blazeward.com/newsletter/

Buy More!
Did you know that you can buy directly from the KRP website?

https://www.knottedroadpress.com/shop/

Connect with Blaze!

Web: www.blazeward.com
Boundary Shock Quarterly (BSQ):
https://www.boundaryshockquarterly.com/

ABOUT KNOTTED ROAD PRESS

Knotted Road Press publishes dynamic fiction set in exotic locations and unique non-fiction voices in genres such as autobiography, business, cookbooks, and how-to. Our authors cover a wide range of genres including science fiction, fantasy, mystery, literary, and poetry, appealing to all readers. We offer both DRM-free ebooks and print books for a global readership.

Knotted Road Press
www.KnottedRoadPress.com
www.KnottedRoadPress.com/Shop